PALMER ENTITY

ASYLUM SERIES BOOK 2

Written by David Longhorn
Edited by Kathryn St. John-Shin

ISBN: 9781099231544
Copyright © 2019 by ScareStreet.com

THANK YOU AND BONUS NOVEL!

I'd like to take a moment to thank you for your ongoing support. You make this all possible! To really show you my appreciation for purchasing this book, I'd love to send you a full-length horror novel in 3 formats (MOBI, EPUB and PDF) absolutely free!

Download your full-length horror novel, get free short stories, and receive future discounts by visiting www.ScareStreet.com/DavidLonghorn

See you in the shadows,
David Longhorn

PROLOGUE

"What's that?" asked Dwayne, stopping suddenly so his friend walked into him.

"Keep the noise down!" hissed Warren, shoving Dwayne aside. The bag of tools Dwayne was carrying clinked, prompting shushing and a jab in the ribs from Warren. "This is supposed to be a stealthy recon operation, not a—a bloody mess."

Dwayne peered ahead of them, into the trees. It was a moonlit night, but he was not used to such darkness. It felt like the countryside, and he was a city boy. They were moving through what seemed like a huge forest, not the small clump of trees they had seen by daylight. Warren was small, wiry, agile, slipping between the trees in near silence. Dwayne was stocky, short-legged, and clumsy, and did not like rough country.

"There's something in front of us," Dwayne insisted. "In the trees. I think it's an animal."

"Probably a fox," said Warren, dismissively. "Or maybe a badger. Nothing to worry about. Come on!"

Dwayne stood watching as his friend pushed on through the damp undergrowth. He knew Warren would simply leave him, so he followed after a couple of seconds. He was sure what he had seen was far bigger than a fox.

"How big are badgers?" he whispered.

"About a medium-sized dog," replied Warren dismissively. "They're not dangerous, they avoid people. Don't you know anything about wildlife? Come on, for God's sake! Don't keep lagging behind."

Dwayne stumbled over something, thought it was probably a tree root. They were still not in sight of the actual building they had come to explore. The trees seemed too dense. He wished he could use his torch, but Warren had been firm about that. The security guard on the gates was out of sight, as they were approaching the apartments from the rear, but someone else might see a light and report it.

After all, Rookwood had attracted a lot of attention for reasons Dwayne did not like to think about. He had protested when Warren had first outlined the plan. But his clever friend had poured scorn on Dwayne's fears. Only kids and idiots, apparently, were scared of ghosts.

"It'll be dead easy," Warren had assured him. "We just get inside, have a quick look around, work out how much wiring we can rip out and sell. Copper's selling for three or four quid a kilo now. And I know this bloke with a van who can help us shift it."

"But what about all those people who died?" Dwayne had asked, plaintively.

"Accidents, and maybe some murders," Warren had shot back. "No such thing as ghosts, bud. Grow up! And man up!"

The way Warren had told it in the pub earlier that day, they were going to make easy money with a couple of nights' work. Dwayne, always short of cash, had agreed to help his friend. But he had not realized that climbing over the wall would be so difficult, or that they would have to trek through a forest. He was sure he had seen something big among the trees. It had been caught in a patch of moonlight for a split second, but when Dwayne had blinked, the dark shape had gone.

"Are there deer in these woods?" he asked.

Warren stopped.

"Deer?" he demanded. "We're in the suburbs, in the grounds of a posh apartment block. There're houses all the way around this place. How could deer get here?"

Dwayne, now resentful of Warren's condescending manner, raised his voice again.

"I saw something with antlers," he insisted. "Like a deer. It was big as well."

"Bollocks," jeered Warren, speaking at normal volume now. "You

2

saw tree branches, they look like antlers. Branches waving in the wind. Now, come on!"

Dwayne muttered resentfully as he thrashed clumsily through the underbrush but decided not to continue the argument. By the time they got to the edge of the trees, he was scratched and bruised and damp. But then they were out of the forest and the dark, blocky shape of their objective loomed ahead of them.

"Okay," hissed Warren. "Keep quiet, keep low—stealth, right?"

Dwayne gave an affirmative grunt. They stole forward, Dwayne trying to move like an action movie hero sneaking up on the baddie's lair. Moonlight reflecting from one of the upper floor windows suddenly dazzled him. At the same moment, he thought he saw someone looking at them around the nearest corner of the building.

But it can't be a person, he thought. *Not with horns. It must be tree branches in the wind, like Warren said.*

They reached the rear wall of Rookwood, and Warren led them along to the left, to the East Wing. This section of the building had been fire-damaged before it could be properly refurbished, he had explained. The doors were covered with hardboard, easy to pry off. Seconds later they were indoors, in near—total darkness.

"Right," Warren said, flicking on his flashlight. "Careful, don't go into any of the rooms facing the front gate, or the security guard might see."

"I know!" retorted Dwayne, resentfully. "He won't be looking up at the building though."

"Unless he leaves his little kiosk for a smoke, or a pee," Warren pointed out. "Now come on, let's see how much wire there is."

As they made their way into the East Wing, Dwayne noticed a faint tang of burning in the air. The fire had happened nearly a year earlier, but the smell suggested a much more recent blaze. He shrugged off the thought, tried to concentrate. Warren was, as usual, giving orders and supervising, waiting for Dwayne to do the actual work.

"Just rip some wiring out of the skirting board," Warren said. "So we can get a look at it, take a sample back to Fat Eric."

Fat Eric, Dwayne knew, was a dealer in scrap metal with a sketchy reputation. The man was reputed to be very rich. Warren had talked about making thousands of pounds.

But how much of that will I see? Dwayne thought, as he laid out his tools. *Warren never cuts me a fair share.*

"Get on with it!" Warren urged.

Dwayne picked up a claw hammer and smashed the wooden skirting board, then ripped away a few feet. The wiring inside was less easily handled. Even though the power was supposedly out, Dwayne made a point of putting on rubber gloves. Warren fretted impatiently, but still did not offer to help.

"Hurry up, doof, it'll be dawn soon!"

Always bullying, Dwayne thought, resentment growing stronger. He cut away a length of wire and jerked it out of the wall. The bare metal shone brightly. Warren snatched it out of his hand, examined the plunder. Dwayne shivered, suddenly feeling cold. He saw Warren's breath as his so-called friend ordered him about, telling him to rip out more wire.

"No," said Dwayne.

The simple word surprised them both. Warren stood looking down at his old schoolfriend, mouth open, as if seeing Dwayne for the first time. The cold became more intense, but it stopped mattering to Dwayne. He stood upright, hammer in hand, a chorus of voices in his head.

'*He'll always rip you off,*' the voices said, chiming in with his own long-festering resentment. '*He thinks you're a moron. False friend! Bully! Smug bastard!*'

"Dwayne, mate, what's up?" asked Warren, his voice suddenly quiet, concerned.

Dwayne raised the hammer. Warren retreated but collided with a stack of empty paint cans and fell backward. Dwayne heard the voices urging him forward, telling him to strike home. He brought the hammer

4

down. Warren, squealing in terror, brought up his hands to shield his face. The hammer hit Warren's fingers, glanced off, but did enough damage to elicit a howl of pain. Warren's flashlight spun across the room, sending crazy shadows hurtling across the bare walls.

"What are you doing?" Warren screamed, scrambling ineptly away on his backside, right hand useless. "Stop!"

For a second, Dwayne hesitated. He recalled the good times he and Warren had enjoyed. But then the voices in his head became one. It was clever and persuasive, and the good times faded.

'This is your chance to get rid of him forever!'

Dwayne smiled, strode purposefully toward Warren again. But the slight pause had given Warren the chance to get to his feet and scramble for the doorway. Dwayne lashed out with the hammer, missed, and was off balance for a moment. Warren reached inside his jacket, and Dwayne remembered the smaller youth carried a knife. Sure enough, there was a click and a thin blade shone in the torchlight.

"Don't make me cut you, man!" Warren warned, taking a fighter's stance.

'He's a coward, a little weasel—you can take him,' the voice reassured Dwayne. *'Besides, you smashed his good hand.'*

It was true. Warren wielded his flick-knife with his left hand, while his right dangled uselessly. Dwayne lashed out with the hammer again, but despite his handicap, Warren dodged, slashed, cut Dwayne's cheek. He felt the warm spill of blood, felt rage, and lashed out. Warren dodged again, but less successfully, and the hammer connected with his forearm. The knife clattered to the bare floorboards. Dwayne closed in for the kill, but Warren lunged forward under the flailing hammer, and head-butted Dwayne. Unable to swing the hammer, Dwayne dropped it and grappled with Warren.

Confusion followed as the young men punched, kicked, and bit each other. Dwayne managed to get on top and tried to throttle his foe. Warren managed to gouge one of Dwayne's eyes with his thumb, escaping the bigger youth's grip. Then both of them scrambled for the knife.

***

Warren looked down at his hands in the bleak, white radiance of the flashlight lying on the floor. The right was crippled, fingers bent sickeningly out of shape. The left hand was covered in blood, as was the knife it clutched. He reeled back and leaned against the wall, trying not to look at the bulky figure sprawled, face up, on the floor.

Dwayne was still breathing, wheezing rather, but Warren knew he wouldn't be for long. A dark stain was spreading around his head and shoulders, blood pumping from the wound in his thick neck. At that moment, Dwayne made a horrible noise in his throat and fell silent. Warren had often wondered what the old-fashioned term 'death-rattle' meant. Now he knew.

'You'll never get away with this,' said a voice in his head. *'No way. Fingerprints everywhere. Even if you get rid of the knife, they'll get plenty of evidence. They'll put you away for a long time.'*

Warren tried to ignore the voice, to devise ways he could get away with it. But every possible path seemed to end in the same way, with the clang of a door you couldn't open from the inside. Warren started to cry.

"It was self-defense!" he whimpered.

'Nobody will believe that,' said the cold, clear voice. *'They'll say you went barmy and killed him.'*

Warren realized this was true. There was no reason for what had just happened. All the stories about Rookwood were true. The place itself was insane, and so was anybody who got caught by it. With that realization came another; it was intensely cold, so cold that Warren was shivering.

'Better end it now,' declared the voice. *'Join the rest of them, here, where you belong.'*

The room vanished, along with Dwayne's body, and Warren saw

Rookwood as it had been. It was a place of fear and pain. Brutal, grinning attendants wheeled struggling patients along bleak corridors to a special, terrible place where monstrous experiments were conducted. Warren felt as much as saw all this, experienced the misery and madness that permeated the building.

"No!" he breathed.

He had a last-ditch impulse to survive, to banish the vision, flee Rookwood, take his chances outside. But then he felt the arm that held the knife moving. He tried to stop it, but it swung up, turned the sharp, blood-stained blade, pointed it at the side of his neck. Warren exerted every fiber of his being to try and stop the metal reaching his flesh. But then came the first prick of pain, and his quivering hand slowly drove the knife into his throat.

The last thing he saw as a living human was the face. It looked as if it was formed out of shadows on the wall in front him, a dark visage that stared at Warren, and appeared to see through him. The face that flickered briefly into existence was human enough to have an expression. It showed a little pity, a small trace of compassion, before it vanished again.

Warren's last thought before dying was of a remark made by the friend he had just killed.

He was right. It did have antlers.

CHAPTER 1

"She thinks we're gay, you know."

Paul Mahan looked up at Mike Bryson, baffled at the Englishman's remark.

"Who thinks we're gay?" he asked. "And if this is some kind of lewd joke, I will not be amused."

Mike jerked a thumb over his shoulder, indicating the living room window.

"No joke, I mean Mrs. Ratbag over the road. Mad cat woman. Curtain twitcher, always looking into other people's business."

Paul laughed, put down his iPad.

"Well, two young-ish men sharing a house, it's a reasonable assumption. And to be fair, it's a little more reasonable than assuming she's called Mrs. Ratbag."

"History will vindicate me," Mike prophesied in a portentous voice. "Anyway, the curry's nearly ready. Prepare yourself for a culinary treat."

"Oh, I'm prepared."

Paul got up and walked to the window. Sure enough, the elderly woman was peering out at them. He waved to her cheerily and she withdrew, fading into the shadows. A gray cat on the window ledge remained, peering inscrutably at him.

"Cats," said Paul. "I forgot about the goddamn cats."

He turned to see Mike looking concerned but trying not to.

"Remember the missing cat posters around Rookwood? Never got to the bottom of that. I mean, did the cats simply run away because of the evil aura, something like that? Or were they, you know, killed in some way?"

Mike shook his head.

"Look, you shouldn't be dwelling on it," he insisted. "Put it in the past. Think about anything else. Work. Booze. Watching terrible old movies. The forthcoming festival of curry flavors."

The Englishman headed back to the kitchen and Paul looked out again, met the green, unblinking gaze of the cat.

If any animal has psychic powers, it's the feline, he thought. *They see things people can't.*

The old lady who was definitely not Mrs. Ratbag appeared again, this time looking down the street. Behind her, another figure appeared, and Paul saw the face of an elderly man, bald and wrinkled, dressed in a cardigan, shirt, and tie. The old man was watching the woman, but she seemed unaware of him. The cat, however, looked up at the man, thrashed its tail, and jumped off the windowsill out of sight.

"Mike," Paul called. "Is Mrs. Ratbag married, do you know?"

"Widow," Mike shouted back. "Bloke in the corner shop told me he died a couple years back. Why do you ask?"

Paul watched the old man fade, become a kind of three-dimensional shadow, his features turning colorless, then blurring.

"No reason," he replied, watching the ghost vanish.

Paul's phone chimed and he checked the caller, sighed. He thought about sending it to voicemail, then decided it would be unproductive. The woman who wanted to talk to him was nothing if not persistent.

"Hi, Mia," he said, walking back to the sofa. "The answer's still no. Thought I'd save you some time by making that clear."

Mia Callan was the producer, director, and driving force of a British TV series called *Great British Hauntings*, or GBH for short. For months, she had been asking Paul to contribute to a special feature on Rookwood. He had no intention of ever returning to the place or going anywhere near it. He had explained this, at length, to Mia via email, Skype, phone, and in person when she waylaid him outside the Humanities Department of Tynecastle University.

"I can offer you a substantially bigger fee, Paul," she began. "It took some negotiating with the money guys, but they finally caved."

Paul smiled, recalled his first and—he sincerely hoped—only meeting with the ambitious young woman. Mia Callan was working-class British, forging a career in a media world dominated by the children of privilege. She took no prisoners, and clearly had no intention of taking 'No' for an answer. Her determination to make an episode about Rookwood might have been admirable in other circumstances. But as things stood, Paul found it irritating, at best.

"Sorry," he said, keeping his voice even, determined to sound sane, reasonable. "It's not a question of cash. It's an evil place, Mia. Nobody should go there. And no, I won't go into details as to why. The press reports, the inquest—that should be enough for anyone. We're not talking about quaint English spooks here. It's an evil place. Stay out of it."

Mia laughed, a slightly shrill sound, almost a cackle. Paul wondered if she was wound up tight all the time, if she ever relaxed. She was one of those people he could imagine never actually sleeping, merely dozing between production meetings.

"I've done far too many shows about quaint English spooks," she said scornfully. "Weeping nuns, headless coachmen, ghostly children crying—they never bloody well turn up, anyway. I want something with a bit of raw meat."

Paul's patience was fraying. His thumb strayed towards the End Call icon.

"You'll get more than you bargained for if you go to Rookwood," he warned. "Seriously. I've got to go."

Before Mia could protest, he cut her off. He waited for her to call him again, but after a few seconds, concluded she had given up. For now. He tossed the phone aside. He knew the producer was pestering other people who had encountered strange, deadly phenomena at Rookwood. He almost hoped one of them would agree to her crazy scheme—spending a night in the abandoned building.

"Come and get it," shouted Mike. "This is one serious curry, best confine it to the kitchen area."

Paul had to smile. He was grateful for everything Mike had done to help him since his traumatic experiences at Rookwood. His friend had seen that Paul should not live alone and had not hesitated to give up his own bachelor pad for a new, bigger place. Both men knew this was because of the risk that Paul's depression, never far away, might start to overwhelm him again. But Mike, typically British in his desire to avoid anything too sincere, had never explicitly said as much. Instead, he had made house-sharing into a big adventure for two overgrown teenagers, eager to have 'lads' nights in', enlivened by beer, curry, and trashy movies.

Thanks, mate, Paul thought, sniffing the distinct odor of Chicken Madras. His phone rang, and he sighed. It was almost certainly Mia Callan again. Paul decided to let it go to voicemail, then changed his mind, picked up the phone. It was not the producer, but someone he had not spoken to in nearly a year. Mike appeared in the doorway, framed by clouds of steam, making a 'What's Up?' gesture.

"Neve?" Paul said. "Is something wrong?"

As he listened to the woman, he realized something was very wrong indeed. He ended the call with a sincere promise, then asked Mike if the curry could keep.

"Sure," Mike replied, throwing a tea towel aside. "Who was that?"

"Neve Cotter," said Paul. "She wants to talk to me."

***

Mike gave Paul a lift across town and parked on a quiet, leafy road. The houses were old, well-built, but somewhat shabby. What had been the properties of the well-to-do were now subdivided into rental apartments. There were plenty of For Sale and To Let signs.

"I'll wait in the car," Mike said. "If you need me…"

"Thanks," said Paul, getting out. "I'll try to keep it short."

He walked along, looking at house numbers, glimpsed a face at a window. It was a young face, curious, probably that of a living person.

He had tried to estimate how many ghosts he had seen since his traumatic time at Rookwood. It worked out at roughly three or four a day, usually brief sightings. In a big, old city like Tynecastle, that did not seem like a high number.

But it's still too damn high, he thought. *Zero would be a more comfortable figure.*

Paul found the right address and, after checking the usual labeled buttons, was buzzed in. The Cotters' flat was on the first floor, the front door decorated with a hand-lettered sign reading 'Ella & Neve Live Here'. Its cheeriness was in marked contrast to Neve's expression when she let Paul in.

"I'm so scared," she said, running a hand through her tangle of red hair. "Scared they'll take her away from me."

"Why?" Paul asked, then felt stupid. "No, sorry, I understand. Have her teachers asked questions?"

"No, but they will eventually, and then how can I explain the marks?" Neve went on. "I keep making excuses for not sending her to school when—when it happens. But they'll run out of patience eventually."

"How long has this been going on?" asked Paul, keeping his voice low.

They were talking in the hallway of the Cotters' small apartment. Paul could see it wasn't as pleasant as the one the mother and daughter had had at Rookwood. The death of Neve's abusive boyfriend, followed by a disastrous exorcism, had driven the Cotters out. But it seemed the ghost called Liz, having established a kind of friendship with Ella, had somehow been drawn back to the child.

"I noticed some marks not long after we moved out," Neve explained. "But they disappeared after a while, and I assumed that was it. But lately, it started happening again. And she wants to see you."

Neve's expression showed clearly that, if it had been up to her, Paul would not be there.

"Did she say why?" he asked. "I only spoke to her a few times."

"Best that you talk to her," Neve sighed. "I don't know what else to do. She's in the living room."

Ella Cotter was sitting, knees drawn up, in an armchair. She was facing a TV with the sound turned low. A nature documentary was on, but Ella was watching without obvious interest. She looked up at Paul and smiled. He smiled back, but felt hollow, slightly sick. The girl was pale and thin, a shadow of the child he had briefly known the previous summer. In her frailty, she looked much younger than her eleven years. Ella was hugging her knees, the long-sleeved shirt she wore riding up to reveal a few inches of forearm. Paul saw that each wrist was circled by a red welt.

"Hi, Ella," he said quietly.

He sat down opposite her, folded his hands. Neve Cotter stood by Paul's chair, both adults ill-at-ease. He was used to talking to students in their teens and early twenties but had had always felt slightly awkward around children.

"Your mom told me—you've had some problems."

"It's Liz," Ella confirmed. "She keeps coming back. She doesn't want to hurt me, or anything. But she keeps coming back. I wish she wouldn't."

Paul thought carefully, choosing his words. He did not want to refer to violent events, either those of last year, or the original mass death at the old asylum.

"Do you know why she keeps coming back?" he asked finally.

Ella shrugged, and he felt a pang of guilt. He had formed an odd, somewhat disturbing relationship with Liz, the most powerful of Doctor Palmer's many victims. Liz alone had resisted being absorbed into the collective entity Palmer had become after the asylum fire in 1955. In a clumsy, intuitive way, Paul had helped free Liz from the purgatory of Rookwood. He had assumed she would move on to some higher plane, or perhaps simply to nothingness.

I should have known it wouldn't have been that simple, he thought.

"Is she here now?" he asked.

Ella nodded.

"But she won't talk to you unless mummy goes away," the girl said matter-of-factly.

Paul looked up at Neve Cotter, who seemed about to reject the suggestion. Then the woman shrugged irritably and walked to the door that led into the kitchen.

"I'll be next door," she said needlessly.

As soon as the door closed, the temperature in the room plummeted. The television picture vanished in a haze of snowy static. Ella's breath was now visible, and her respiration was faster, shallower than seemed right. Paul moved to sit on the floor next to the girl's chair, examined her wrists.

The red welts grew darker as he watched. He could see traces of buckles as well as straps impressed into the child's flesh. It was hard to tell in the dim light, but Paul also thought he could make out marks on Neve's head, just behind and above her eyes. The stigmata of psychiatric abuse sickened him, and he was angry that restraints and electrodes last used before he was born should still inflict suffering on an eleven-year-old girl.

"Liz," he said quietly, but emphatically. "You're hurting her. I don't believe you want to do that. You helped protect Neve and Ella, we both know that. Why make her unhappy now?"

Ella gasped, and her eyes rolled up into her head. Paul's heart raced and he was about to call for Neve when the girl reached out, put a finger to his lips. The white eyes seemed to peer into his. Then the small, pink lips opened.

"Paul," rasped a weak, feminine voice he knew well. "I'm sorry. I'm very sorry. They always told me I was a bad girl. Wicked. And now I'm doing a bad thing."

"Then why do it?" Paul demanded. "Why not move on? You met your daughter, your baby, and that freed you from Rookwood, didn't it?"

Ella's eyes rolled back into place. They were green eyes, like her mother's, and seemed huge in the small, pinched face.

"Yes," said Liz's voice. "It let me escape for a while. But not—not completely."

Paul was baffled. But then he thought of the ghosts he had seen, the faded presences who haunted places they had known in life. There were so many who had not 'moved on', to Heaven or Nirvana, or perhaps simple oblivion. But he had always assumed, like the husband of Mrs. Ratbag, a soul lingering on the earthly plane must have something to anchor it. What could keep Liz here? Only one possibility occurred to him.

"Is it Palmer?" he asked.

He instantly regretted the question. Ella Cotter quivered, her head wobbling alarmingly, and a thin trickle of drool flowed from the corner of her mouth.

"Yes," Liz said finally. "He's getting stronger, and there's a link to him I can't break. I think it's to do with—with some bad things I did. I don't think I'm allowed to be free until I put something right. But I don't know how!"

Paul reached out, wanting to hold Ella's hand, but then hesitated. He was afraid to touch someone else's child, especially when they were alone together. Liz, however, had no such reservations. She grabbed his hand with both of Ella's, leaned forward, and the temperature in the room dropped another degree or two.

"What did you do that was so wrong?" he asked.

The girl's hands gripped his so tightly he almost cried out in pain. The strength in the child was abnormal, so much so he feared her own fingers might get damaged—torn ligaments, even broken bones.

"I killed Palmer," she hissed. "I murdered him with the power he gave me, murdered him without touching him. Killed him with my mind. And I enjoyed it, because he drove me mad, took away who I was so he could make me his—his pet, his creature."

The girl leaned back in her chair, letting go of Paul's hand. He felt a slight diminution in the intense cold. The more emotional Liz became, the more energy she seemed to draw from her environment. Again, he wondered if she had given thought to the harm she might do to Ella. Paul took a deep breath, forced himself to make an offer.

"Liz," he said, "you—you took control of me before. You can do it again. Leave this girl, she's not part of this. You want to communicate, fine, but do it through me if you must use someone. Let me try and help."

Liz laughed through Ella. It was horrifying, far more chilling to Paul than any fall in temperature. The laughter was borderline crazy in its intensity, revealing a mind that was in danger of losing control. He wondered if Liz had deteriorated since her partial liberation from Rookwood, if the revelation that she was not wholly free threatened her precarious stability.

"It's not you I want, Paul," the girl rasped. "If I can't be free of this world, then I want to live the life I should have had. I want my life back! The one they took from me when they took my baby away! I don't want to be a ghost anymore."

Paul stared at Ella's face, into the great, dark pupils of those perfect green eyes. Ella was clever, loved, and probably had a long, interesting life ahead of her. Ella would live in a world where she could aspire to be almost anything and was bright enough to achieve a great deal. She had a connection to Liz, who had been denied everything except rape by a depraved uncle, a shameful pregnancy, and a few months as Palmer's human lab rat. And then death. To Liz, Ella's world must be immensely tempting.

"I—I can't blame you for wanting to live," Paul said carefully. "But you have no right to take Ella's life from her, to deny her freedom. She's done nothing wrong—"

"I DID NOTHING WRONG!"

The scream was all the more terrifying because of the way Ella's face grew red with rage, her eyes bulging, spittle flying from her mouth. Along with the outburst came a juddering vibration that rattled ornaments, and a book fell from a shelf on the far wall. Neve Cotter hurtled into the room, rushed over to her daughter, grabbed the girl. The mother darted a venomous look at Paul.

"What have you been saying?"

Paul struggled to make himself heard as Ella continued to shout.

"I did nothing wrong! I want to live! I don't want to be dead!"

It took a few seconds for Neve to grasp what Liz was saying through her child. When she did understand, she reeled back, almost falling. She stared at Ella in horror, then glared at Paul.

"She's possessed!" the woman cried, crossing herself. "You've made it worse, you stupid bastard!"

"Liz," Paul said, trying to sound stronger than he felt. "Liz, let her go. Let her go, and I'll help you be free of Palmer, of Rookwood."

Ella's body became rigid, and she fell silent. Then Liz's voice, querulous and pleading, spoke again.

"Don't let him get any stronger," Liz said. "If he gets much stronger, he might come alive again, alive in a strange way. I don't understand, I don't understand—"

Ella slumped, her eyes closing, and again Neve enfolded her child in her arms, sobbing in fear and confusion. Paul wanted to ask more questions, but felt the chill begin to recede. Condensation on the window near Ella's chair was vanishing.

Liz, he thought, *has left the building.*

***

"Well," remarked Mike, as he wove his battered Peugeot through the early evening traffic, "that couldn't sound more ominous, could it? What did she mean, 'come alive again'? Possession, the way Liz took control of the little girl and you?"

Paul did not reply immediately, staring out at the streets, watching people go about their normal, sane lives. Tynecastle was a party town, famed for its nightlife. Every winter, if it snowed in England, national newspapers showed pictures of Tynecastle girls in skimpy dresses and high heels, 'braving' the weather. Already, groups of young people were in evidence, making their way between the city center pubs. He thought he glimpsed one of his own postgrad students, a brilliant girl with a bright future.

Then he thought of Liz, consigned to a mental hospital for being impregnated at fifteen. He remembered how drab and thin she had looked when she had manifested herself at Rookwood. He imagined the tormented, lonely ghost drifting through the crowds of laughing, tipsy girls, girls who had opportunities and freedoms unimagined in Liz's day. They could say what they liked, wear what they liked, make love to whomever they chose. It wasn't a perfect world by any means, but to Liz it might seem like a Utopia.

Of course, the girl would seize upon the chance to have a do-over, he thought.

"But two wrongs don't make a right," he finished aloud.

"Yes, I think you might have cut to the chase there, mate," replied the Englishman. "But I take your point. You can't let Liz take over Ella's life just because she got the dirty end of the stick."

Mike paused to change gear, swerved around a group of young men jaywalking in the familiar British style, and cursed them under his breath.

"Amazing how close so many people come to death, so often," he remarked. "And how they don't get it. Especially the young. No wonder Liz feels cheated, outraged, wants her share. But she's not entitled to Ella's life."

"No," Paul said wearily. "But I don't see how I'm supposed to help her. What she said about Palmer is disturbing, but it's all typically vague. I get the feeling the afterlife is even more chaotic than this one."

"Makes sense," Mike remarked. "Think how bloody daft people are, how dishonest, self-deceiving, mean. Then add that desperate yearning to not be dead a lot of them presumably feel. It must be purgatory."

Paul made up his mind, at that moment, to tell Mike something he had been withholding for too long. The Englishman had been a good friend, understanding about Paul's issues with depression, always willing to listen to his colleague's woes. He waited until they were stuck at a set of traffic lights and told him the truth.

"Mike," he said. "I've been holding out on you about something that happened to me at Rookwood."

Mike glanced over, gave his trademark, lopsided grin.

"I know," he said. "The way you act sometimes. Like a cat in a Gothic story, staring at things I can't see. Is it—ghosts?"

Paul let out a sigh of relief. It was not the first time he had underestimated Mike's perceptiveness. The Englishman played up to his image of a slightly boozy, lecherous guy, but in fact, he had a keen mind. And, Paul reflected, he had probably been giving out clues that even a dullard would pick up on.

"Yeah," he said, smiling back at Mike. "I see dead people. Dead people like Mr. Ratbag, for instance."

"Kind of makes sense," said the Englishman, after a long pause. "You spent time among powerful, crazy spirits, ghosts, whatever you call them. It would be surprising if something didn't rub off. And I don't blame you for keeping quiet about it. I would have. Keep schtum and hope it gets better—I tend to do the same with toothaches and always regret it."

The lights changed and the Peugeot stalled.

"Oh, sod this heap of junk!" muttered Mike, restarting the motor. "I should have traded it in when it was worth something. Anyway, what does the lovely Doctor Blume think about your ghosts? Symptoms of a repressed psychosis, that sort of thing?"

Paul shook his head, thought about the therapist who had tried valiantly to help him for the past months.

"I was afraid to tell her at the start," he confessed. "And now, after all this time, I'm afraid she'll see it as a kind of betrayal. Proof I'm not serious about getting better."

"Hmm."

Mike turned off the main drag, hit some speed bumps. They drove on in silence for a while.

"Tell the truth and shame the devil," Mike said finally, as they entered the street where they lived. "She probably hears stranger things. Ghosts are a bit mainstream these days. And here we are, home again."

They parked on the street and got out. Paul saw the old lady opposite peering through her net curtains. There was no sign of anyone else behind her. The big, handsome cat was dozing on the windowsill.

"I can unfreeze the curry, if you like," Mike said, then gave the neighbor a big wave, prompting the woman to move out of sight. "Curses, I wanted to slap your bum while she looked on. Do you think she knows? About her old man?"

"She might have some idea," Paul said. "But I'm not about to ask. The cat knows, that's for sure. And yeah, let's have that curry. But no inappropriate touching!"

Later, having eaten, they opened a couple of beers and continued to discuss Paul's options. The first, Mike pointed out, was to get the hell away from Tynecastle and Rookwood, maybe return to the States.

"If not that," Mike said, "then why not try for a job in London? Put a few hundred miles between you and all that paranormal craziness."

Paul admitted he had often considered the 'just run away' option.

"But I know I'd feel like a coward," he explained. "I got involved by accident, sure, but it's unethical to wash your hands of other people's problems once you are involved. You should do your best to help."

Mike grunted noncommittally.

"Okay, you're a secular saint," he said, his tone and expression suggesting he was not entirely joking. "But option two is to get yourself some help and try to find out more about Rookwood. Because at the moment we know flip all about why this kicked off in the first place."

Seeing Paul's puzzlement, Mike continued.

"Think about it," he said, wielding his half-empty beer bottle for emphasis. "Doctor Miles Rugeley Palmer conducted horrific, amoral experiments on mental patients. He tried to trigger paranormal powers, or increase them, with drugs like scopolamine, and electro-whatcha-call-it."

"Electro-convulsive therapy," Paul put in.

"Right, ECT," Mike said. "But from the evidence Rodria unearthed, Palmer seems to have succeeded beyond all reasonable expectations. I mean, it was the Fifties, all sorts of grossly unethical research was underway in the Soviet Union, and the West. Sad to say, but the things Palmer did weren't so widely different from documented experiments elsewhere. Yet Rookwood is now haunted by this Palmer entity. If there's anything else like it out there, I've not heard of it. Why?"

Paul pondered the question. He had assumed Palmer's grotesque research had been the sole explanation for the haunting. But now he thought about the power of the entity, and that of Liz, and wondered if something else might be at work. He looked at Mike, who had a slightly smug half-smile.

"You already know something, don't you?" he accused.

Mike took another swig of beer and shook his head.

"Not me," he said, "but I know a man who does."

"The last time you recommended I visit an expert, I ended up with Max Rodria," Paul reminded Mike.

Mike, to his credit, looked shamefaced.

"Yeah, that was a bad error of judgment on my part. But Percy is nothing like Rodria—he's an amiable, slightly dotty old chap who retired years ago. No crass ambition, no desire for fame, just an encyclopedic knowledge of British folklore, mythology, all that jazz. And when I called him recently, he said he had some interesting material on Rookwood."

Paul was still skeptical. Seeing this, Mike added, "Also, Percy was my tutor when I was a mere freshman at Tynecastle. He always found time to talk to me about my problems, however dumb they may have been. He's a good man, really."

Paul, still dubious, agreed to meet Percy.

CHAPTER 2

"Ghosts," said Doctor Blume, her voice professionally neutral.

She made a note on her pad, looked up at Paul, an eyebrow raised.

"I guess I should explain," he said slowly. "I told you I experienced strange phenomena at Rookwood? I even consented to hypnosis, and you heard what I went through, right? Even though you didn't believe it."

The therapist nodded and smiled.

"I did not dismiss what you told me," she said. "But, by the same token, I can't accept it as objective fact. Hypnosis does not guarantee accurate recall, despite the widespread belief that it does. You believe it happened, that's where we can agree."

"Well," he went on, "I accept it as very factual. I appreciate how hard you've tried to help me with my depression, and I think I have made progress. But this thing, Rookwood, the Palmer entity, it's been hanging over me like a cloud. Can't go back, can't move on."

After making another note, Blume asked: "Do you see ghosts—often?"

Paul looked past the therapist, tried to focus on the blurred figures moving between Blume and the far wall.

"I'm seeing a few kids right now. Their clothes tell me they were born in the nineteenth century, and you told me this place was an orphanage, right? And before antibiotics and so on child mortality was high, especially in less than perfect conditions. It seems reasonable to conclude they died here and haven't been able to move on since."

For the first time in nearly a year, Blume looked startled. She half-turned in her chair, then stopped, gave a nervous laugh.

"All right," she said. "You see ghosts. But you appreciate that if I don't see them, I can't accept them as real?"

"What if you could see them? Would you accept them as real then?" Paul shot back.

Blume fell silent, raised her pen, then lowered it. No note this time. Finally, she replied.

"If I started to see ghosts," she said, "I would assume I was hallucinating and seek the opinion of a qualified professional. Sometimes, one cannot accept the evidence of one's own eyes."

"You see," Paul said, getting up. "I'm in kind of a Catch-22 here. I need therapy to help me get over mental health issues, and those are related to what happened at Rookwood. Whenever I'm alone, part of me is back there, in that place. Not good. But if I tell you the truth about my experiences, I won't be believed—well, not by anyone with a professional background. And I've seen enough priests and psychics to know they're not for me."

Doctor Blume stood up in turn and tried to dissuade him from leaving.

"You've been very patient," he said, trying to ignore the dead orphans peering up at him with huge, dark eyes. One was reaching up to tug, in vain, at the hem of Doctor Blume's jacket. "But I need to work this out for myself, somehow. The talking cure is fine, but—I need to act, to do something."

"Do you know what you'll do?" she asked, as he opened the door.

"No," he admitted. "But I know where I have to go to do it."

When Paul reached the sidewalk, he phoned Mike Bryson.

"This expert of yours," he said. "Would he appreciate a bottle of brandy, something along those lines?"

***

Lancelot Percival was, Paul ascertained, a man of many qualifications. Apart from his regular BA he was also an MA, a Ph.D., and D. Litt, as well as being a Fellow of the Society of Antiquaries. The

Society was a venerable organization, founded in 1707, and not noted for its tolerance of cranks. This was promising. When Mike drove them to Percival's home Paul was surprised to find it was in a streamlined, modern block of apartments, rather than some ivy-covered parsonage. And when the old man answered the door, Paul finally relaxed, and decided to confide in the retired expert.

Percival was much as Mike had described him; a small, very thin man, who looked as if he had no surplus flesh on his bones. He wore glasses with a chain around his neck and kept polishing them with a pale cloth in, what Paul assumed was, a nervous gesture. Percival spent the first few minutes of their visit puttering about, offering them tea, expressing delight at Paul's gift of moderately-priced cognac, offering them tea again. Eventually, they decided to have tea, plus some Battenburg cake. Percival disappeared into the kitchen, and Paul heard the clink of crockery. The apartment showed signs of having been cleaned and tidied at some point, but Percival was clearly one of those readers who allowed books to colonize every available surface.

"His daughter comes in to check on him every week or so," Mike said quietly, as they cleared reading matter from the couch. "His wife died a few years ago. He says he doesn't mind the single life, but I think he enjoys visitors. He's a natural lecturer, apart from anything else."

Percival reappeared with a cake stand and plonked it on a coffee table in front of his guests.

"Now," he said, rubbing his hands together. "I understand you have had some less than pleasant encounters at Rookwood, hmm?"

"That's right," Paul replied, "but I guess Mike has already told you—"

He stopped as the old man raised his hand, an apologetic expression on his face.

"Michael has his virtues," Percival said, "but he does have the British gift for understatement, something Americans seldom indulge in. I really would like to hear the story from the horse's mouth, while we wait for the tea to brew."

Paul spent the next few minutes trying to describe what happened after he moved into Rookwood. Occasionally Percival would interrupt, apologizing for 'breaking the flow', to ask a detailed question. Paul revised his opinion of the old man. While Mike's old professor seemed a little vague at times, he was clearly knowledgeable and perceptive. After Paul had finished, Percival rubbed his hands in satisfaction.

"Quite a splendid narrative," the old man said. "Terribly upsetting for all concerned, of course. But I think I have the spoor of this Palmer entity of yours. Yes, yes indeed, it seems we have a very unusual phenomenon here."

Then Percival scuttled out into the kitchen again and returned with a laden tea tray. After pouring out three cups of Earl Grey the old man settled himself in a battered easy chair and crossed his skinny legs.

"Rookwood," said Percival. "The name is itself significant. Members of the crow family are traditionally associated with dark forces, and of course, they are very clever birds—always grounds for suspicion, you'll find. Rooks, thanks to their habit of gathering in vast numbers, were believed in olden time to hold actual parliaments, passing judgment on malefactors. Like ravens and crows, rooks were long associated with the dead, and some thought them to be psychopomps."

Paul struggled to recall the meaning of the word, held up a hand to stop the old man explaining it.

"I remember now," he said finally. "Heralds of the dead, who usher the soul to the afterlife."

"Very good!" exclaimed Percival. "There's hope for your students, young feller me lad. Now, as to the actual location of your—well, your unpleasant experiences, there are a few records that give me pause for thought. For instance, there is this chap..."

The retired professor bounced up out of his seat and crossed to a bookcase, ran a hand along assorted volumes, journals, and pamphlets. Paul could not see any order to the way printed matter was arrayed on the shelves. But Percival still found what he sought, pouncing on a slim booklet with bird-like precision.

"Aha, yes! This is it."

Paul took the proffered booklet. It had the unpromising title, *Pagan Sites in the Northumbrian Region*. He flicked through it, stopped at an illustration. It was evidently an old woodcut and was captioned 'The God of the Witches'. Paul guessed it was a Victorian artist's conception of how witchcraft had been practiced. A group of robed women, all quite young and attractive in a bland way, were dancing around a shadowy figure. The god was, perhaps deliberately, hard to make out. It consisted mostly of a roughly man-shaped block of darkness. But there were two bright eyes, and a set of impressive antlers.

"A pagan nature deity?" Paul asked, indicating the picture.

"Quite so!" replied Percival. "And also associated with Rookwood, interestingly enough. There are many variations on the theme, of course. Cernunnos was the Celtic horned god, while the Greeks had Pan, bringer of panic. That is a common feature, by the way—the god inspires fear, often to extremes, but is not necessarily evil. But to medieval Christians, of course, the horned god was synonymous with Satan. One could say he got very bad press, disproving the idea there is no such thing as bad publicity."

Mike took the booklet from Paul, guffawed at the woodcut.

"Looks like a bunch of New Age hippies at a festival, just before the magic mushrooms run out."

Percival wagged a finger at Mike.

"Michael, you were a good student, but prone to facetiousness, as I believe I noted in the margins of several assignments. The point is this rather dark and mysterious deity was linked to Rookwood, long before the asylum was built."

"Are we talking about legends, folk stories?" asked Paul.

"Not entirely," returned Percival, gesturing at his chaotic library. "There are some well-attested accounts of people shunning that area, even quite recently, in historical terms. People wouldn't live there, and local farmers left the woods alone. Charcoal burners would normally have felled the bigger trees, but they kept well clear. Gypsies, or Roma if you like, did not camp out near Rookwood. They clearly knew something."

"Surely somebody owned the land?" put in Mike. "They must have done something with it."

Percival smiled, darted off to his shambolic bookshelves again.

"They tried to," he said, as he started to rummage. "Usually, it was simply trying to exploit the timber. But they ran into difficulties. Local men would not work there, labor brought in from elsewhere quickly deserted. And then, around 1900 if memory serves, a crisis arose. Ah yes, here it is: Extracts from a clergyman's journal."

The old man sat down again, leafing through a battered hardback book.

"Here," Percival said. "Listen to this, from 1897. '*The young Lord Staindrop finds himself in great financial difficulty, due to the imposition of death duties on his father's estate. It seems likely he will have to sell most of his holdings, including the Rookwood land. This will, of course, cause concern among the locals. Villagers have already approached me, asking if I might possibly influence his lordship so as to avoid any trouble. When I ask what this trouble might be, they are vague. But one oldster warned that 'the one who walks in the trees' would not be pleased if the wood were tampered with. I fear, however, when Tynecastle grows, it will inevitably impinge upon this neighborhood. With what consequences, I cannot tell.*'"

The professor paused, looked up at his audience.

"Is that it?" asked Paul. "Vague intimations of trouble?"

"Ah, no!" exclaimed Percival, again riffling through the yellowed pages. "I think there is another—yes, here it is. This is a privately printed book, essentially the journal of a local clergyman. It has a few entries relating to our subject, albeit buried in less interesting fare. He writes that the process of selling Rookwood took over a year because there were no local buyers. But an investor from London was found and took the land off the young lord's hands for a relatively small sum. Staindrop was clearly desperate. And then the fun really started. There was a plan to cut the wood down to build an exclusive housing development, which failed. Then a sanitorium was proposed, but that plan fell through. The local priest is somewhat vague as to reasons, but then—well, here, look at this passage."

Paul took the decrepit volume, handling it carefully, and peered at the small, spidery print. The page began with some typically British remarks about bad weather and the high price of groceries. Then the clergyman moved on to the 'difficulties with Rookwood'. It emerged that plans to build a sanitorium had foundered on local opposition and a series of mishaps. The plan had been altered, and now the proposed building was to be an asylum. What happened next was briefly summed up.

Cutting down most of the trees was eventually accomplished, but only by paying the men twice the normal rate and bringing in outsiders from over the Scottish border. No locals would provide accommodation for these workers, again adding to the expense, as the company had to erect large tents and provide other facilities. There were a number of unfortunate accidents, all of which were attributed to 'the old one' or 'the Wild Huntsman'. This un-Christian conviction that some preternatural being haunts and guards the woodland is as deep-rooted as any such belief. I have preached against it but cannot seem to shift the superstition.

And now there has been a death. A surveyor from London was apparently working alone in the woods early morning on Tuesday, when a sudden hailstorm set in. When the man did not return to the workmen's camp, a party was sent out to search. They found the poor fellow with his back to a tree, eyes wide with horror, hands constantly in motion. It was as if, one of the searchers told me later, the surveyor was continuously trying to push something away—a thing that had clearly subjected him to such a terrible, panicked fright that he died before the night was out. The physician diagnosed no injury or illness, merely the after-effects of some awful shock. The man was not old, but they say his hair had turned pure white.

And yet, it seems, the tree felling will continue regardless, until most of Rookwood is destroyed. The asylum will be built on the bare earth that remains...

Paul stopped reading, looked up from the journal.

"Is that it?" he asked, unable to hide his disappointment.

But Percival was already back among his books, reminding Paul of a squirrel in pursuit of a pinecone. The third item he found was a bulky book that might have been a photograph album. But when Percival opened it, Paul saw it was an old-fashioned but once vital research tool—a book of newspaper clippings. Percival laughed when he saw his guest's expression.

"Yes, we're back to the Stone Age, or at least the world before Googling."

He put the book down on a table that was already well-laden with reading matter, clearing a space by the simple expedient of sweeping a few other books onto the carpet. Then he searched through the pages of yellowed newsprint until he found the item he was looking for. Paul looked over the old man's shoulder and felt a flutter of apprehension when he saw the headline. *ROOKWOOD ASYLUM HAUNTED?*

A former attendant at the asylum has claimed a terrifying presence has been glimpsed in the East Wing of the building. The asylum, which opened in 1906, has been dogged by claims of strange apparitions. Some have claimed a tall figure with horns (or some kind of bizarre headgear) has been sighted in and around the institution.

However, the director of the asylum has dismissed such reports as mere rumor, often originating in the delusions of inmates. This newspaper has often received reports concerning unusual and disturbing events at Rookwood, which has seen many staff members depart suddenly and for no adequately explained reason...

The report ended inconclusively. Paul noted the date of the report was 1922. He flipped forward through the collection of clippings. There were a couple of more reports from the same decade, then one dated 1933. After that, however, Rookwood was not mentioned at all. Then, in 1955, he came across a series of items about the fire that almost destroyed the East Wing and killed most of the staff and patients. There was no mention of any paranormal phenomena, however.

"I don't get it," he said. "It seems like the weird stuff kind of tailed off before Palmer took over. Why should that be?"

Percival closed the album of clippings and cast it casually aside, leaned back in his battered leather armchair.

"What is a god?"

The question took Paul by surprise and he laughed, then felt slightly ashamed. Percival's expression was full of gentle reproof.

"That's a little above my pay grade, Doctor Percival," Paul replied. "Maybe if I get tenure, I could form a coherent viewpoint."

"I'm quite serious," said Percival. "Our ancestors had no doubt deities existed, beings we now consign to reference texts and learned theses. But once, human beings every bit as sane and intelligent as ourselves made offerings to the manifold gods of the forest, the stream, the thunder. What were they, these ancient gods?"

"Anthropomorphism," Mike said, surprising Paul. "You taught me that. So-called primitive people attribute purpose to things we explain through physical laws. They had gods for all the important things, like fire, hunting, the seasons, and so on."

Percival made a quiet, high-pitched humming sound, and Mike laughed.

"That's his disapproving noise," he explained to Paul. "He thinks I'm being glib, shallow, dismissing a complex issue."

"Quite so!" exclaimed the old man. "The rational explanation for the beliefs of so-called primitive peoples is that they were dogged by fear, superstition, a desire to explain everything in terms of essentially human motivation."

Paul nodded, wondering where this might be leading.

"The sky god is furious with the sea god because the sea god stole his lunch money, so there's an almighty storm, that kind of thing?"

"Yes, precisely," said Percival. "But, despite your slightly facetious tone, you have made it quite clear one ancient superstition—the survival of consciousness after death—is fact."

Percival smiled brightly and jabbed a thin finger at Paul.

"Which leads me to ask, what if a few other ancient beliefs have a core of truth?"

"Now you're being kind of dismissive and glib," Paul protested. "Sorry, but the Palmer entity, the whole Rookwood thing, is not a conventional haunting. It seems bound up with Palmer's experiments, which were essentially scientific. Perverted science, maybe, but still science."

To Paul's surprise, Percival clapped his hands briefly, eyes twinkling.

"Good, good, we are having a real discussion!"

But not a very helpful one, Paul thought. However, for Mike's sake, and out of politeness, he decided to keep going.

"So," he said slowly, "are you saying it's precisely because a scientific institution was built on the site that this—deity, forest spirit, whatever, kind of faded away?"

Percival shrugged.

"Perhaps," he said. "But perhaps not. It could be that destroying most of what had been sacred land did the trick. It is much easier to believe in a nature deity when there is a large, dense forest for it to lurk in. Whoever said gods could not exist without people to believe in them was not far wrong, I think. What remains of the actual Rookwood is now a rather meager belt of trees. The rooks are still there, however. And perhaps something else lingers. Something Palmer, unwittingly, managed to supercharge with his experiments. A force of nature, but one the doctor perverted and tainted with his monstrous behavior."

Paul suddenly felt very tired. He had spent a near-sleepless night wondering what he could do to help Ella Cotter, preferably without risking his life. He was not in the mood for intellectual jousting, no matter how amiable Percival was. The fact that the little man obviously wanted to help only made all the talk of pagan superstition more frustrating.

Perhaps sensing Paul's mood, Percival sat looking at the American for a few moments before nodding. When he spoke again, it was in a more serious, measured tone.

"I think we should cut to the chase, as they say," explained the old man. "I think Rookwood is a place of ancient, somewhat obscure power, and perhaps that power has been revived and refocused by Palmer. It's taken him a while, I suspect, but he's getting there."

"Okay," Paul said, "accepting that argument for now, what is it that makes Rookwood so special? I mean, where does this power come from in the first place?"

Percival jumped up again, but this time did not dart to his bookshelves. Instead, he pointed to one of the volumes he had consigned to the floor a minute ago.

"Michael, if you would? *The Old Straight Track*, I think."

Mike gave Paul a mock-martyred look and bent to pick up the book. He held it up for Paul to see.

"You familiar with this bloke? Alfred Watkins?" asked Mike. "No? Well, I'm not surprised. His ideas have been widely discredited."

As Paul took the book from Mike, Percival tutted at his former student.

"Throwing the baby out with the bathwater, Michael. Just because some of his ideas were wrong does not mean Watkins is not of interest. And he had something to say about Rookwood."

Paul examined the book, checked the publication date—1925. The blurb on the back cover referred to ancient routes called *ley lines*, a vaguely familiar term. He looked up at Percival.

"Is this something to do with what's called *earth energy*—the idea that the planet naturally generates some kind of paranormal field at particular places?"

"It is," Percival confirmed. "It was a very popular idea in the Sixties, for obvious reasons. Believers hold that a typical sacred site dating from the Stone Age originally became significant because psychic phenomena occurred there. They were places where the gods dwelt, in part because people believed they did. The expectation created the deity, in a sense. There was a process of synergy, or feedback. And it was when worshippers stopped believing, for whatever reason, that the old gods, like old soldiers, began to fade away. But, it might be argued, they did not all fade away at the same rate."

Paul sat and pondered the idea for a while.

"Okay," he said finally. "Let's accept—just for now—some kind of being—call it a god, spirit, whatever—was genuinely present at Rookwood. And the Palmer entity is tapping into the same primeval forces that created it. Where does that get us?"

Percival leaned forward and smiled, but thinly, without his usual cheer.

"It may be," he said, "that Palmer is trying to become a god. It certainly would accord with what we know of the man's character. Quite an egotistical chap, by all accounts. A very limited deity, in terms of space—hardly omnipresent. But powerful, nonetheless, and essentially immortal."

Paul reflected on the dark, cold being he had encountered at Rookwood. He remembered the cruel, amoral power Palmer had marshaled in death. Percival's ideas, wild by conventional standards, did not seem so strange when set against the evil that clearly dwelt in the former asylum.

"The old gods give way to the new," said Mike. "All hail the Palmer entity."

For the first time, Paul could detect not a hint of facetiousness in his friend's words.

***

"Would you like some cocoa, poppet?"

Ella Cotter looked up at her mother, nodded. Neve felt a wrench of despair, tried to keep her smile fixed. In the past, she might have turned to the church, but after events at Rookwood, her faith had been undermined. She did not dare take Ella to the doctor, in fact, was terrified a regular illness would make it necessary. Reaching out to Paul Mahan had been, she felt, an act of desperation. All it had done was frighten her and subject her daughter to more torment.

When Neve brought the cocoa back into the living room, she noted, with relief, that Ella had taken out her sketchpad. Ella had always enjoyed drawing as a little girl but had stopped when they moved into Rookwood. A few months earlier, she had raked out her pad and pencils and started sketching again. She had produced some excellent pictures of insects and other 'minibeasts' that inhabited the small back garden. Neve had stifled her usual distaste for bugs and encouraged Ella to keep it up.

"What are you drawing, sweetie? More creepy crawlies?"

Ella shook her head.

"No, just stuff."

They sat quietly for a while, sipping their cocoa, and then Neve said it was 'time for bed, young lady.' Neve resisted the urge to hover around Ella, giving her daughter space, suppressing her fear that Liz would return. But she insisted on kissing Ella goodnight, something she had not done in three years. Once, the girl would have insisted she was too old for that now. But on this night, she did not protest.

Leaving Ella's bedroom door ajar and the hall light on, Neve went back into the living room and tried to work. She could not focus on her web design jobs, and soon gave up in frustration and disgust. Slamming her laptop shut, she went to the couch to watch TV. But as she groped for the remote, she noticed Ella's sketchpad. It had been left on the floor by the armchair, along with an array of pencils.

If untidiness was the only thing I had to worry about, she thought. *God, that would be paradise.*

She got up and gathered the drawing materials, took them over to the table. As usual, she could not resist looking at what Ella had been working on. When she turned back the page, she froze. It was a picture of Rookwood.

"Oh, God."

After the shock had subsided, Neve examined the drawing more closely. It was good, if basic, showing the building from an unusual angle. Neve worked out the point of view was of someone hovering near the main gate, or slightly to one side. From this perspective, one could see the actual woods behind the apartment block. The trees were rendered roughly as a blur of branches, with no sign of leaves. Evidently, the time was winter.

We moved in during April. She never saw the place in winter. Of course, she could have imagined that. Given what we went through, it makes a kind of sense for her to imagine Rookwood during the bleakest time of the year.

But there was something else, which Neve found genuinely odd. There was something in the woods, a barely visible form. Neve peered more closely, but could not decide what the creature was. Not a deer, she decided, despite the fact its antlers were the best-defined feature.

Perhaps a man in some strange costume? Or an exotic breed of animal rearing up on its hind-legs? The more she stared at it, the more disturbing it seemed.

She flipped the sketchpad closed, laid it down, and went back to the sofa. She fell asleep watching a mindless action movie with the sound turned down. She woke after midnight from a dream in which she was being hunted through moonlit woods by the creature in Ella's sketch.

CHAPTER 3

Paul's visit with Lance Percival had not helped him make up his mind. But memories of Ella Cotter's suffering preyed on him so much he felt he ought to do something, rather than sit back and wait for events to unfold. Participating in Mia Callan's TV show would at least give him the opportunity to find out more.

"And I could help in a practical way," he said to Mike. "If anything does start to kick off, I could urge them to get out before things get worse."

They were walking through a small park near Tynecastle University, taking a breather after lunch. All around the edge of the small square of greenery, the city traffic roared by, the midday rush hour at its height. The academic year was coming to an end. Paul still had plenty of work to do but was struggling to focus on it. He explained to Mike that perhaps facing Rookwood again could prove cathartic.

"Why not go the whole hog," Mike said, "and try to undermine the entire TV thing? Plant doubts in their mind, try to scare them into not going. Or at least give them the jitters so they won't hang around."

Paul was impressed by the simplicity of the notion. Mia Callan wanted him to give some kudos to her show by featuring an articulate, intelligent witness to the phenomena at Rookwood. All she wanted him to do was tell the truth, about how terrifying and destructive the Palmer entity was. Paul reasoned that, given the death toll and other disturbing events, this might be enough to deter Mia, or at least other members of her team.

"Hey," Mike added. "Don't these production companies have insurance? Aren't they required to assess risks and all that jazz? Surely if there's a real danger to life, limb, or sanity they have to pull out?"

"Good point," Paul replied.

He was about to speculate further when something caught his eye. It was a pleasant day in early June and the neat little park was full of people enjoying the sunshine. A group of students was having a picnic nearby, or at least they had spread a rug, laid out some food and drink, and were now all silently absorbed in their phones. Paul had to smile, pointed out the scene to Mike. He began an observation on the way social media made people less sociable. But he forgot what he was saying in mid-quip.

Now a semi-circle of figures stood around the picnickers. They were a family of four, evidently parents and a boy and a girl. Paul could not see them clearly in the noonday sunlight. But from their clothing, he guessed they had lived, and died, in the early to mid-twentieth century. One of the students looked up from her phone, and Paul recognized her, waved. She waved back, returned to her emails or texts. Behind her, the dead family stared down forlornly at the untouched picnic. A male student, who had taken off his shirt, frowned and put it back on, though there was no breeze, and the sun still beat down strongly.

"How old is this park?" asked Paul. "I mean, what was here before it?"

Mike looked surprised, then led him to the park's main entrance, gestured at a plaque.

"As Sherlock Holmes said to Watson at some point, 'My friend, you see but do not observe.' You must have walked past this dozens of times."

Paul read the plaque, which explained the park had been built on the site of a block of homes destroyed by bombing during World War Two. 'Thirty-eight people died, among them fourteen children.'

"You're still seeing the dead, then?" Mike asked.

Paul nodded, looked round for the picnic party. He saw them getting up, packing their stuff away. The vague outlines of the old-time family shimmered in the sun, then vanished. He glanced around, trying to make out other ghosts. But after a few moments, he gave up, unable to be sure in some cases.

"It could be a lot worse," he thought. "I could have ended up like Ella. I have to try and help her, find out how to defeat Palmer. But—but, in this case, it looks like the bad guy holds most of the cards."

They strolled back toward the university on the opposite side of the park.

"He seems to," Mike concurred, rubbing his chin in thought. "But remember, Palmer is trapped in that empty building. So what's his endgame, his ultimate objective? To get out the way Ella did? Because he tried that and failed."

"Yeah, but people will keep going to him," retorted Paul. "That's the way it is. People will not leave that place alone, so all Palmer has to do is wait. Percy is right about that, Palmer is accumulating power. If only there was some kind of weapon, something we could use against him."

Mike was silent for a few moments, then spoke again.

"Maybe I'm being really dumb," he said, "but isn't your friend Liz the obvious weapon to use? She killed the guy, after all. She has enough power to defy him. If she wants your help, the least she can do is pitch in on your side."

Paul could not fault his friend's logic.

"True," he said, "but she's not what you'd call reliable. I'm not sure she'd even talk to me, now, except through Ella. Which I can't see Neve accepting. She's not my number one fan."

They left the park and crossed the busy street, then entered the university campus. They discussed everyday topics for a while, until the time came for them to separate, Mike to his English department, Paul to History. At the last moment, Mike started to speak, stopped, then laughed.

"What's so funny?" Paul asked.

"Ah, probably nothing," Mike admitted. "But I was just thinking. Doctor Blume has put you under her mesmeric influence a few times, right?"

"Yeah, but she didn't believe what I told her, or at least not fully," Paul replied. "Why do you ask?"

Mike shrugged.

"It's a long shot," he said. "But since we're in the realms of the spooky... do you think hypnosis might be a way to contact Liz?"

Paul frowned.

"Why should it?" he asked, confused. "She's not some artifact of my imagination—or is that what you're suggesting?"

"No, not at all!" insisted Mike, raising his hands in a placatory gesture. "But you told me you shared her memories, pretty intense ones, which means you were connected on a very fundamental level. And later she actually took over your body, right? Maybe some trace of that connection survived."

Seeing Paul was still skeptical, Mike continued, "Doesn't a medium go into a kind of self-induced trance to contact the dead?"

Paul smiled.

"Yeah, I guess they do," he admitted. "Now tell me how I'm going to persuade Doctor Blume."

***

Doctor Blume was, at first, very resistant to the idea, but Paul wore her down by insisting it would be therapeutic. Then she refused to allow Mike to be present on the grounds of patient confidentiality, and despite several hours of argument, Paul could not get his friend nearer than the therapist's waiting room.

"What makes you think Liz will respond anyway?" Blume asked, gesturing Paul to his usual seat. "If she's a wayward ghost who wants to possess a little girl?"

Paul sat down and took a breath.

"I don't know if she'll react at all," he confessed. "But when I lived at Rookwood, she was quite friendly, if a bit erratic."

Paul had provided the therapist with a list of questions to ask Liz, assuming she appeared. He had also outlined just who Liz was, or had been. Doctor Blume, predictably, had concluded the girl was an artifact of Paul's imagination, but agreed to treat her as if she were an independent being.

"Assuming she turns up," she added. "Now, Paul, if you'll just try and relax, we'll see how it goes."

Paul looked around the room.

"You can try the couch," said the therapist, "or just your usual chair. Either is fine, I'm not going to try anything we haven't done before."

"Okay," said Paul, sitting down, recalling the relaxation technique she had taught him.

He gradually unwound as the doctor talked. It was a familiar script, telling him to think of a beautiful place where he felt safe, warm, happy. His mind went back to a family holiday before his mother got ill. He was sitting by the shore of Chesapeake Bay, working his toes in warm sand, watching distant sailboats. It was a moment of perfect peace, careless and dream-like.

The sound of waves and wheeling gulls did not drown out the voice of the therapist. She was counting backward. And then she was asking a question about a girl, a girl Paul vaguely remembered meeting. In fact, he had met her somewhere in England, which was weird, because when had he been there? He smiled, not at all fazed by the paradox. This was a happy time.

What was her name again? Oh yeah, he thought. *Liz.*

The sky darkened, the sound of the water and the birds faded away. A gust of wind, cold and fierce in its intensity, blew up the beach. Color drained from the view, and the tiny sailboats disappeared. There was no sign of life, the sunlit shoreline replaced by a bleak vista. Then Paul noticed there was someone else on the shore, a small, slender figure walking up the gray beach toward him.

"Hello Paul," said Liz. He noticed she sounded British. "You wanted to talk to me?"

"Did I?" he said, peering up at her.

"Yes," she said, sitting down next to him. He noticed she was not dressed for a day at the beach. She was wearing a dull-looking dress, worn shoes. Liz was thin, thinner than Paul, and she seemed older than him, and sad. Her face, he thought, might have been kind of pretty with those big dark eyes, but she was too drawn and tired looking.

"Liz, can you help Paul?"

The woman's voice, which had an accent like Liz's, seemed to come from the colorless sky. They both looked up, then at one another, and giggled.

"That was weird," he said.

"It was," Liz agreed. "But I can help you. If I really wanted."

"Why wouldn't you help Paul? Isn't he your friend?"

The cold wind grew stronger, icy, and Paul shivered. Liz frowned up at the invisible questioner, then looked down at the gray sand.

"I would like to help," she said. "But I don't want to be caught in that place again. I don't want to face Palmer again, after spending all that time fighting him. And—and there's something else. Something even scarier than Palmer."

Paul knew the name Palmer was significant but could not remember why. He could tell from the way she whispered the name, however, that Liz knew all too well how bad this mysterious Palmer was.

"What is scarier, Liz? What frightens you more?"

"Nothing!" the girl shouted, jumping up.

The beach seemed to buck and heave, the sky flickered with a kind of colorless lightning, then tore apart. Paul stood next to Liz, still wearing his beach outfit, feet bare. Now he stood on grass, and the color of the world had been restored. In front of them was a building he recognized from somewhere. Behind him, he heard a distinctive sound, a harsh cawing from dozens of birds.

Rookwood.

With the name came terror. Paul felt himself lifted off his feet and carried forward, skimming the grass, toward the building. He tried to fight the force that was moving him, but this just meant he thrashed clumsily at the chilly air. He was approaching the entrance, the great double doors gaping, the interior dark and apparently empty. But the emptiness, he sensed, was watchful, and hungry.

"Liz!" he shouted. "Liz, help me!"

Paul looked down and saw he was no longer a boy, but a grown man. He was powerless, though, as the remorseless, invisible force took him inside Rookwood. He shouted for help again, pleading with Liz to come with him, save him. As he drifted out of the sunlight, he heard her voice, the words just barely audible as he plunged into a darkness that wanted to make him a part of itself.

"Paul? Can you hear me, mate?"

Mike Bryson was looking down at him, shaking him by the shoulder. Paul blinked, wondering if Doctor Blume would object to Mike intervening. Then he saw the therapist crouched in a corner of the room, face white with shock. The office was a shambles, papers and framed certificates scattered around, chairs overturned, the doctor's desk standing askew.

"I think Liz got a bit worked up," Mike explained, helping Paul to his feet.

Only then did he realize his own chair must have moved at least a yard to one side.

"The doctor's PA wanted to call security, or the cops," Mike went on. "When she heard the uproar, she thought you were attacking the doc. I managed to persuade her to call paramedics instead. She's downstairs waiting for them. I think your therapist is going to need the kind of help she provides."

Doctor Blume looked up, her expression still confused and scared. The men went over to her and helped her up. The therapist peered at Paul, eyes wide, and seemed to struggle to speak. When she did, it was in a small, frightened voice.

"She's real. She really exists. I can't pretend she doesn't."

They managed to tidy up the office before the paramedics arrived. Doctor Blume was checked over, found to be physically unharmed, and rejected an offer to be taken to see an ER doctor.

"I am a doctor," she insisted. "And I choose not to be admitted to hospital."

After leaving Blume's office, Mike asked whether the experiment had worked. Paul tried to describe what he had experienced, and how he interpreted it.

"She said nothing scares her more than Palmer?" Mike asked, as they got into his car. "So why should admitting that upset her so much? We sort of knew already, yeah?"

Paul shook his head.

"I think she meant she fears nothingness more than Palmer," he said. "She fears nonexistence, oblivion. That's the whole problem with this 'moving on' notion. What if there's nowhere to move on to? No Nirvana, or heaven, just a final extinction of the individual?"

Mike eased the Peugeot out into traffic as Paul mulled over the other thing he had learned. Liz was conflicted between going near Rookwood again and her desire to help him. In reply to his final, desperate plea in his trance, she had given the best commitment she could.

"I'll try my best, Paul," she had said. "I promise you, I'll try."

***

Paul met the television team near Rookwood. Vehicles were parked by the Grey Horse. The group had agreed to have a pub lunch, and a general discussion of the show's format, for Paul's benefit. When he entered the main room, he spotted Mia Callan's bright purple hair immediately. Even if he hadn't, he would have heard her voice. She was petite, around five foot three, but with a big presence and an infectious laugh.

"I knew you'd come around, Paul!" she said, as always talking just a little more loudly than necessary. "This is going to be great, one of the best episodes. And with you on board, we've got that authentic feel we need—and you being American won't hurt our chances of selling the show to the states."

She introduced Paul to the other members of her team. The cameraman was Joe Durham, a shaven-headed forty-something with a stocky frame and a matter-of-fact approach. Joe struck Paul as a veteran who regarded this job as just another paycheck. Laura Blaine, the sound engineer, was a cheerful woman of about twenty-five. She had worked with Mia from college onward. All three greeted Paul with varying degrees of enthusiasm. The same could not be said for the star of the show.

Lucas Sharpe had made his name as an actor in an Eighties police procedural show. He had played the handsome, dynamic Inspector Grist for eight seasons. After the show had ended, however, Sharpe had failed to get any more significant roles. He still retained some of the good looks that had helped his career, but if he ever had much charm, Paul felt it had pretty much run out. Sharpe was in his early sixties, set in his ways, and clearly resented sharing the limelight with anyone. Paul found himself staring at the white rings around the actor's eyes, where presumably he had protected himself from tanning product.

"Another amateur, eh?" he bellowed, pumping Paul's hand with loud, obviously fake bonhomie. "Don't worry, lad, I'll keep you straight, make sure you don't embarrass yourself."

The man's manner, while unpleasant, did not worry Paul as much as the distinct whiff of booze he caught when Sharpe spoke. Paul wondered if he had a drinking problem, then thought it might be a good thing.

If he falls flat on his face in the middle of shooting, he mused, *that might help get them out of the damn place.*

He realized he had missed something, as the others were looking at him.

"Sorry," Paul said, "I was lost in—unhappy memories."

Sharpe snorted, knocked back most of a double whiskey. Mia jumped into the conversation, ever eager to direct events on or off camera.

"Okay, Paul, that's the introductions over with," she said. "Next, I thought we could just run over the basics—how you got there, what you experienced, your theories about it all. Filmed against a suitable background, of course."

Twenty minutes later they were outside the gates of Rookwood. The interview went much as Paul expected, in terms of questions. He had long since given up prevaricating about what had happened. Sharpe proved to be one of those actors who could remember his lines when half-drunk, and the scripted questions—provided by Mia—were competent enough. It was only when they came to the question of risk that things became difficult.

"How dangerous do you think this particular haunting is?" asked Sharpe.

"I sincerely believe anyone going into that place is putting their life at risk," Paul said. "I know it sounds ridiculous, claiming a ghost has killed people. But we're not talking about a conventional haunting, if there is such a thing. Miles Rugeley Palmer has become the core of a kind of entity, a being with uniquely powerful and dangerous attributes. Just look at the evidence!"

"Cut! We can use that, great stuff," called Mia.

"I hadn't finished," Paul protested. "I would like to talk about the specific instances..."

But Sharpe was already turning away, clearly happy his stint was over, and planning to go back to the pub. As the actor walked down the road Mia smiled indulgently, while Laura rolled her eyes at Joe.

"Don't worry, Paul," Mia said. "The magic of editing means we can record some more remarks from you, splice it all together later. There are quite a few things I'd like to ask, as it happens. Okay, we're rolling, Laura? Joe? Right. For instance, Paul, couldn't everything that happened be attributed to non-supernatural causes?"

Paul sighed.

"Yes, the police did a great job of rationalizing everything. A mentally unstable workman who'd been bullied turned a drill on the guy tormenting him. A violent man stalking his ex-girlfriend and her daughter fell out of a window during a struggle. And then they claimed Max Rodria, a guy with a doctorate in physics, somehow electrocuted himself with a portable gasoline generator."

"An accident like that is perfectly possible," Mia put in.

"Yeah, but eyewitnesses don't support the mundane explanations," Paul retorted. "I saw Jeff Bowman fly out of that window—he was thrown by some kind of force, he didn't fall. I saw Rodria killed by something that tore the cables free and wrapped them around his body. And then there was the priest, and the professional psychic..."

Again, Mia interrupted.

"And yet, in every case, there's very little video evidence."

Paul shrugged in frustration.

"There's footage of Imelda being strangled with her own necklace," he pointed out. "There's some phone footage of Rodria being attacked— poor quality, maybe, and yes, people always claim these things are fake. For every believer, there's at least one denier. But I've yet to see any convincing account of how the images were supposedly faked."

Mia nodded encouragingly as she posed another question. Her whole approach reminded Paul, to her, showbiz came first.

"What about the mysterious Liz?" she asked. "The former patient at the asylum? Do you still have any contact with her?"

He hesitated. He was well aware that claiming to have spoken to a ghost had not helped his career. He always tried to focus on Palmer, treating Liz as a kind of bit-player in the story, a sad ghost who had helped him understand the danger Palmer represented.

"I—I have spoken to her recently, yes," he admitted.

Mia looked delighted, as well she might.

"And is she around now?"

"No!" Paul insisted. "It's not like that, I'm not a medium or something. I just—I happened to make a connection with what you might call a ghost."

"And why do you think that was?" Mia asked. "Why you, and not somebody else?"

Paul stared at her. The question had caught him by surprise, though it was obvious enough. He thought back to his encounters with Liz, before he had been sure she was not an ordinary girl. The gaze of Mia and the unblinking eye of Joe's camera seemed to bore into his soul as he struggled for an explanation.

"Could it be," Mia asked, her voice slightly lower than usual, "you were as lonely and unhappy as her?"

The implication was that Paul and a dead mental patient were kindred spirits. He shook his head, deciding to bring the interview to an end. At the same moment, Laura Blaine gasped, clutched at her headphones, lifted one off her ear.

"Jesus!" Laura muttered. "I got some tremendous feedback there."

Joe lowered his camera.

"I got something there, too. Could have been lens flare, not sure. Shouldn't be a major issue."

Mia paused for a moment, then decided to end the interview.

"These location shoots always have a few gremlins," she told Paul. "Or maybe you think it's one of your ghosts?"

Before he could reply she pressed on.

"Anyhow, it would be better to get some shots of you inside, preferably walking up to the place. You know the kind of thing—Paul Mahan returns to Rookwood for the first time since the strange events, and so on and so forth."

Paul shrugged. He was still hoping the show would be aborted. As they trooped back to the pub, he raised the question of insurance, trying to sound casual. Mia had a ready reply. Insurance firms did not take the paranormal seriously as a threat. The only real issue was that Rookwood's East Wing had sustained some fire damage, but it was not considered serious.

"What about the deaths?" he protested. "Don't they take them into account?"

Mia smiled indulgently.

"As you said, the police explained all the deaths in rational terms. Mentally unstable people, plus some bizarre accidents. Yes, I know, there were a few oddities, and that's what we'll emphasize in the show."

Seeing his expression, she put a hand on his arm in an attempt at reassurance.

"I know you've had a hard time," she said. "Believe me, I've worked with traumatized people before. But if things look like they're getting a bit too risky, we'll bug out. You have my word on that."

***

"Has she gone?"

Ella looked up at her mother, sitting opposite at their kitchen table, and made her familiar thinking face. Then she nodded.

"Yes, I think she's gone," said the girl. "I don't hear her anymore. And I don't feel the cold she seems to live in."

Neve began to ask a question, but Ella anticipated her, putting down her lunchtime sandwich, and holding out her arms for scrutiny. Bending over, Neve examined Ella's wrists. The red welts, echoes of Liz's restraints, were almost gone. A casual observer would not notice them.

A good teacher would notice them, though, Neve thought. *And that's what matters.*

"That's good," she said, trying not to sound too excited. Liz had departed before but had always come back. "Do you think—she might be gone for good?"

The girl shrugged.

"She comes and goes," Ella said. "She's not very disciplined. I don't think she had much of an education. She doesn't seem to know anything about science or history. And she seems upset a lot of the time. I suppose being dead all this time doesn't help."

Neve had to smile at her daughter's courage and matter-of-factness. Most adults would not be coping so well. While pale and underweight, Ella was already livelier than she had been the previous day. Neve broke a rule and offered her daughter a piece of cheesecake with her lunch. Ella looked startled, then accepted.

"I'm not really ill, you know," she added, as Neve opened the fridge to get the treat. "I'm just tired."

"I know, poppet, but you've been brave and deserve a reward."

In between mouthfuls of cheesecake, Ella started to chatter about familiar, everyday subjects, like the upcoming summer holiday. It was a great relief to Neve that school would be out, so she would not have to fake reasons to keep Ella at home if Liz came back. But she still felt apprehensive. She had little confidence in Paul Mahan, despite the American's obvious desire to help. He seemed to her just another man making promises, and she had known too many of those, beginning with Ella's worthless dad.

I could be wrong about Paul, she told herself, as she sipped her tea. *He is taking a big risk.*

"Is Paul a good man?" asked Ella.

Neve, startled, set her mug down. Sometimes Ella seemed able to read her thoughts.

"I think he tries to be good, but gets a bit confused and scared, maybe," Neve said slowly, not wanting to speak ill of people to her daughter. "He's trying to help, so he is a kind man, I think. And of course, he's quite bright. For a man."

Having polished off her cake, Ella took a drink of tea from her long-time favorite Kermit mug, and Neve braced herself for another question.

"So why don't you like him?"

Neve smiled wearily, knowing she could not evade her offspring on this point. Ella had a remorseless way of questioning you until you either lost your temper, or simply told the truth. And Neve was not going to lose her temper.

"I don't dislike him or anything like that, poppet," she said carefully. "I just think he's rather sad, lonely, and—and maybe a bit weak."

Ella pondered that as she took another bite of her baguette.

"Yes," the girl said finally. "That's what Liz thinks, too. She likes him, but she doesn't think he's brave enough to do—"

Ella frowned again, her thinking face more intense. Neve felt her heart racing, tried to keep a normal demeanor.

"Brave enough to do what? Does she want him to do something dangerous?"

Ella stared into her tea, shrugged.

"I can't remember. It's all fuzzy in my head now. When she's not around I sort of half-remember things she said. Or things she thought. It's weird."

Ella took another mouthful of tea. The conversation was apparently over, at least on the topic of Paul. Again, Neve contemplated the man. He was not her type, with his sandy hair, slightly absent-minded manner, and above all, his tendency to wear denim shirts and corduroy jackets. He struck her as nerdy. She had always preferred more assertive, confident men.

Yeah, and look how well that's been going lately.

"Paul's friend Mike is quite nice," Ella remarked. "He might be fun."

Neve stared at her daughter, then laughed, a little too loudly. She would not normally relish a conversation about her relationship drought, but it was preferable to discussing the paranormal.

"Mike? Are you trying to set me up with a bloke who wears little gold chains on his shoes, and probably calls women chicks?"

Ella wiped her mouth carefully with a tissue and put it neatly next to the remains of her lunch.

"No," she said, "I just think we should both get to know more nice people. Fun people. And then you won't become sad and lonely like

Paul."

Well, Neve thought, as she collected the plates. *That escalated quickly.*

***

Lance Percival's cleaner had just departed, leaving him in his usual state of anxiety. The woman in question was kind, thorough, and charged reasonable rates. But she did have a regrettable tendency to tidy things away, put books back onto shelves, and even throw out what she regarded as 'junk'. So, rather than inspect the quality of her work in the bathroom or kitchen, Percival always spent a half hour after her weekly visit making sure nothing too drastic had happened to his beloved books.

"Oh dear, the poor thing," he muttered to himself, as he rescued a volume that had been shelved upside down. He then found *The Old Straight Track* had been moved from the coffee table onto a totally unsuitable shelf and chuckled at the kind of mind that could confuse folklore with theology.

"Forgive them, Lance, for they know not what they do," he found himself saying. "But sometimes I despair of our educational system."

Then Percival stopped his counter-tidying and stood up straight. An idea was worrying at the back of his mind. The retired professor knew better than to try and force his aging brain to cooperate. His subconscious had its own ways and means and would not be bullied. Instead, he adopted his usual trick of doing something utterly unconnected to his lifelong research.

First, he turned on his radio, which his daughter had tuned to a local, easy listening station during her last visit. It was just on the half-hour, so the regular diet of 'classic' pop gave way to a brief news bulletin. Percival half-listened to the usual political nonsense, which made so little sense that he had long ago given up trying to understand it. Then the newsreader moved on to Tynecastle news. Percival noted the two teenagers who had disappeared a few weeks ago had still not been found. Police were appealing to the public for information.

"Drugs, perhaps," he said to himself. "So much crime these days."

As a disc jockey's well-practiced cheeriness replaced the fast-talking newsreader, Percival puttered into the kitchen and started to make himself some lunch. He was halfway through preparing a macaroni cheese when the swirling vortex of pasta triggered a thought.

"Whirlpool," he said, stirring the sauce. "Something that draws in, rather than repels. Yet the ancient deity of the woods inspired fear, drove interlopers away. Hmm. Presumably, Palmer wants more followers, worshippers, disciples. Yes. A conflict, there. Clash of forces, old and new. The pagan god was a product of awe and fear, and therefore, shunned. The new god Palmer is attempting to become wishes to inspire terror, yes, but also fascination, reckless curiosity, and so lure more victims. Hmm."

He poured the pasta into a bowl and took it to the table, sat down.

"So, how to resolve it?"

Percival held up a forkful of pasta, watched the dense yellow sauce drip back into the bowl. Then he swallowed it, lifted another forkful, mechanically worked his way through the meal. It seemed to Percival there must be tension between forces old and new, and perhaps this very tension might produce energy, albeit of an unstable kind. He made a mental note to let young Michael know, so he could tell his American friend. If only he could find that fancy phone his daughter had given him, but the cleaner seemed to have tidied it away somewhere.

"Oh well, I'm sure it will turn up sometime."

The old man stood up, took his bowl to the sink, and rinsed it out, then put on the kettle to make a nice pot of Earl Grey. After pouring hot water into the pot he left it to brew and, as was his wont, puttered back into his living room-cum-library. He was currently reading or re-reading at least six books, which were scattered around the place. His method was simply to pick one up as he passed by, read a few pages, then put it down elsewhere.

A much-loved book on British folklore caught his eye where it sat askew on the window ledge. He picked it up and opened it to where he had marked his place with a flyer from a Lebanese restaurant. He walked slowly back into the kitchen, skimming through paragraphs, then paused. He stood in the doorway, Earl Grey forgotten, staring at a sentence he must have read a dozen times before. It read:

> *Various Celtic gods were linked with Roman deities following the conquest of what became the province of Britannia. In many cases, a local deity was effectively merged with its Latin equivalent, a practice found throughout the empire. This combining of gods may seem strange to us...*

"Merged," murmured the old man. "Now there's a thought. And not a very happy one. Dear me, no."

He began to search for his phone.

CHAPTER 4

"I went to the city records office," said Mia to Paul, "and made a bit of a nuisance of myself until I got a copy of this old building plan. If you'd like to point out some relevant sites, I'll stay out of the shot while you talk, ostensibly to Lucas."

Mia's tone was neutral, but it was clear she preferred to leave the old actor in the pub for now and record his 'questions' later for dubbing. She spread the large sheet of paper on the hood of the TV team's van. Joe zoomed in while Laura struggled with a stiff breeze, trying to keep her shotgun microphone from wobbling into the shot.

"Okay," Paul said, holding the plan down. "Over here you have the East Wing, which is where the fire occurred back in fifty-five. The main block, here, is where I lived for a short time. As you can see—"

As he talked, he fought a familiar sense of futility, his old enemy— depression—rising up like a dark tide. No matter what he said or did, he felt these people would go ahead and do something dumb. Fresh-faced Laura, old pro Joe, and the dynamic Mia would not be deterred, no matter how often he described death, madness, and terror. And Lucas, old showbiz trouper that he was, would go along with the rest because he had no other career choices.

"... when Rodria's device malfunctioned, we all ran for it. Is that okay?"

"Fine, lovely! Now," Mia went on, "let's go to Rookwood, set up camp. Joe, please go and collect Lucas."

This is it, Paul thought, as he climbed into the van with Mia and Laura. *I'm going back. I swore I never would.*

There was something anticlimactic about driving up the road from the Grey Horse to the gates of Rookwood. A security guard in a small kiosk waved them in after a brief, cheerful chat with Mia. Paul knew she had 'cased the joint', as she put it, several times, and found nothing strange about the old asylum.

They pulled up around the back of the building. After consulting the plans, Mia had settled on a storeroom that had not—so far as anyone knew—seen any unusual events. From there they would set up motion-sensitive cameras and other equipment. Paul had reluctantly agreed to spend some shooting time at the sites of actual deaths or near-fatal incidents. He reasoned, if he co-operated quickly and efficiently, the filming would be over sooner.

The storeroom proved to be empty, its windows small, and made of pebbled glass. It had a bleak, clinical aspect, but the director pronounced it ideal. Mia and Laura worked efficiently as a team, setting up a couple of laptops on a folding table, checking Wi-Fi signals, rating acoustics in the room, then in the corridor, and finally in the foyer at the front. Paul checked his phone, found nothing unusual, then helped do some basic fetching and catching. While he was getting some more equipment from the van, Joe pulled up in his car, along with Lucas. The actor, Paul noticed, was distinctly red-faced.

Wonder how many whiskeys he had before Joe could drag him away?

As soon as the cameraman brought his gear inside, the production team started to check existing footage. Lucas, clearly bored by the whole process, decided to talk to Paul. Like many actors, Lucas Sharpe seemed insecure and soon turned the conversation to his only major triumph.

"I'm told my American residuals are doing rather well," he said. "I've often thought of dear old Inspector Grist as the character who will help me through my eventual retirement."

Paul smiled uncertainly.

"Your show's still running in the States?" he asked. "It's like Columbo and Murder She Wrote, I guess. People love those old-time detectives."

Lucas' expression told Paul he had said the wrong thing.

"I hardly think," the actor began, "Inspector Grist falls into the same category as those rather stereotyped sleuths. No, we always felt the character had a depth, an almost Shakespearean subtlety, that raised the series well above the common ruck of crime drama."

Paul was unsure how to respond and caught an amused look from Joe over Lucas' shoulder as the old actor rambled on. Then the cameraman, evidently feeling sympathy for Paul's plight, waved him over.

"Hey, Paul, come and check this out."

Joe brought up Paul's first interview on the laptop screen. Paul felt he looked unhealthy, pale, slightly manic. But the cameraman was not worried about the interviewee. He fast-forwarded to the end when Mia asked Paul about Liz.

"See, this is where Laura got feedback and I got—well, this," Joe said.

He advanced the film frame by frame. At first, Paul saw nothing unusual. He had been in medium shot, head and shoulders framed against the backdrop of Rookwood on its low hill, just beyond the perimeter wall. Then, as he watched, a gray shape appeared in one frame, jumped rapidly across the screen in the next, then vanished. Joe went back a couple of frames.

"Anyone you know?"

Joe selected the upper-right quadrant of the screen and enlarged it. The grayish shape might have been a human face. Paul could make out two dark blurs and a longer blur underneath, conforming to eyes and a mouth.

"Weird thing is," Joe said, switching to the next frame, "I thought it was lens flare, a bright flash. As you can see, nothing of the sort. It's kind of a dark smudge, not light. I thought it might be a pigeon flying past, but no. It's an image of a kind I've never come across. Now, let's take another look."

When enlarged, the second image was much clearer. It was Liz, complete with her bobbed hair and bangs, her dark, soulful eyes, her pale, pinched face. Paul, trying to keep his voice level, confirmed she had appeared as he was being questioned about her. The others had all gathered round by now, even Lucas, who belched quietly at one point, but said nothing.

"Amazing!" enthused Mia. "That's one of the best ghost pictures we've ever had. Oh, sure, they'll claim it's fake or just an artifact of the digital camera, but who cares? We're off to a good start. Laura, how about you? Was that feedback what it seemed?"

They moved over to the second computer, where the sound engineer began working on complex, and to Paul, baffling, software. Laura isolated what seemed to be a screeching noise, declared it was 'not regular feedback', because the waveform's 'different', and then tried to 'clean it up'. Laura slowed down the screech until it became a rapid gabble, then a chipmunk-like burst of chatter. Finally, she produced something recognizable as speech, though the words were almost obscured by loud background noise.

"Is that her?" Mia asked. "You recognize the voice?"

Paul nodded, not trusting himself to speak. Whatever Liz was saying, she seemed to be trying to shout over the deeper sound that threatened to drown out her words. Laura attempted to clear up the recording and eliminated much of the troublesome noise. She slowed down the words more, over-compensating so Liz's voice was now a deep bass-baritone.

"What's she saying?" asked Mia, who had produced a small camera and was filming Laura's work.

The sound engineer isolated each syllable, piecing the words together.

"Save us..." Laura said, matter-of-factly. "Pretty sure it's 'Save us from' something."

Eventually, she was satisfied with her work.

"Save us from the dark god... Save us from the dark god..."

For the first time since arriving at Rookwood, Paul felt a chill. It was, he thought, purely subjective, but all the more intense for that. He thought of what Lance Percival had said about the pagan deity that had been evicted from the site before the asylum was built.

"Any thoughts, Paul?" asked Mia, swinging her camera around.

"Okay," he said. "Let me level with you."

He gave his account of Percival's ideas, trying to sound as dry and academic as possible. He noticed each member of the team responded differently. Mia was her usual intense self, focusing on every word, asking snappy questions. Laura was quiet and thoughtful. Joe looked a little bored but listened respectfully. Lucas, sitting on a folding chair by the desk, seemed baffled by it all, and snorted at a couple of points.

"That's—amazing," Mia admitted when Paul had finished. "The idea that Palmer's experiments somehow supercharged a primeval force that was present on the site. Yeah, it's a nice twist. I like it. I think our audience will lap it up, especially the Celtic bangle brigade."

She lowered her camera.

"Right, Lucas, this is where we go exploring—we'll hit all the places where major incidents happened. You've got your script?"

Paul was not required for the scene-setting but tagged along rather than be left alone at 'base camp'. They exited the storeroom into the foyer, and he remembered the terrible possession of the medium, Imelda Troubridge. The Palmer entity had almost forced its way out of Rookwood by controlling the hapless woman. But at the last moment, even Palmer's formidable power had failed.

"Right, Lucas," said Mia. "Scene-setting—over to the left a little, that's it, not too far; we'll get direct sunlight…"

As the team set up, Paul looked out through the glass doors at the patch of lawn where Jeff Bowman had ended up, twisted and broken. Bowman had been a stalker with a record of domestic abuse, so Paul felt little compassion for him.

Maybe he deserved it, he thought. *After all, Liz was acting to defend Ella.*

A moment later, an unpleasant afterthought occurred to him.

Was she protecting the child out of goodness? Or did she see Ella as a potential host for her mind, spirit, whatever, even back then? If so, she was simply looking after her own interests.

***

Mike Bryson's phone rang while he was in a meeting with a postgraduate student, and so he let it go to voicemail. When he checked it later, he heard a slightly rambling, confused message from Lance Percival. He called the old man at once.

"Conflict, and tension," Mike repeated, "that's a driving force, a source of energy? Wouldn't the presence of a rival force simply undermine Palmer?"

"It could be," admitted the old man. "But remember we are dealing with somewhat unnatural phenomena."

"We've not really established this pagan deity is still around," Mike pointed out. "He, she, or it, might simply have snuffed it after Palmer came along and stole their thunder. We've seen Palmer's files, and the films he made of his experiments. There's no hint of some other presence in any of those documents."

"A good point," Percival conceded. "However, there is a widespread belief such entities can go dormant—sleep if you like—for long periods. Our putative deity might be stirred to action by Palmer's activity. Then comes the conflict, between the old force that seeks to drive folk away, makes its believers keep a respectful distance, and the new that wants more victims to absorb. And after that may come a merger as the more powerful force subsumes the weaker and takes on some of its attributes."

"Which force would be more powerful?" asked Mike. "Palmer, I'm guessing, because he's already subsumed so many victims, right?"

Percival hemmed and hawed a little over that, but tentatively agreed.

"But," he added, "never forget that older can sometimes mean wiser. Our nameless god of Rookwood could have a few tricks up his sleeve. And Palmer, like all arrogant men, might be impulsive, reckless."

After some discussion, Mike agreed to let Paul know what Percival had said, although privately he could not see how it made much difference. He thought about calling, then decided to text him, in case he interrupted shooting. Then he got back to work. A minute or so later, his phone pinged. He brought up the message and felt a pang of worry.

UNDELIVERABLE

The service reassured him it had tried repeatedly to send the message.

"I'm so grateful," he muttered. "But that doesn't really help, does it?"

After a moment, he decided to try to call. His service provider could not connect him, and was, again, very apologetic. Mike checked the time. He could simply drive up to Rookwood and ask to see his friend. But did Percival's theorizing justify interrupting the production? More mundane tasks demanded his time, and Mike dithered. He tried to contact Paul a few more times but failed.

I'll go after work, he thought. *Won't hurt to check on him. It's not as if he's alone in that place.*

***

Again, Lucas Sharpe proved thoroughly reliable once the camera was rolling. Paul began to appreciate that, for all their differences in age, personality, and style, the old actor and Mia worked well together. Their relationship was something like louche uncle and sensible niece, with a hint of flirtation. But Paul could not pay much attention to the program-making process, as he was permanently on edge as they made their way around the building.

When will it start? Paul wondered. *Will they run for it when I tell them? Can Liz help?*

After some discussion in the foyer, Mia decided to ascend to the first floor and the Cotter's old apartment. This was a relief to Paul, who was dreading any move into the East Wing. He had hoped fire damage might be sufficient reason for them to keep outside, or at least for the team to spend very little time there. He looked past the old caretaker's office, at the entrance to the East Wing. The unlit corridor ended in a vague rectangle of darkness that seemed to heave and writhe as he peered into it.

Probably just imagination, he told himself.

"Paul?"

He turned his attention to the director and followed her up the stairs. Once in apartment 112, she positioned him with his back to the window, the one through which Liz had hurled Jeff Bowman. Paul felt a tingling between his shoulder blades as he prepared to answer much the same questions as they had covered before. Later, Mia would select the best takes and, 'splice it all into a wonderful, coherent whole.' Or so she said.

"I still think it's dangerous just to be here," he put in, feeling it might become his mantra. "I know you're skeptical, and you've every right to be. But I'm convinced there's a very real, very evil presence here. And if that sounds crazy, so be it."

Mia made a circle of thumb and forefinger, grinning broadly. Behind her, Lucas was frowning at his phone. After checking with Joe and Laura that they had got what was needed, Mia briskly moved on to the next job.

"Right, we're going to check out the East Wing, people," she said. "And before you say anything Paul, it is a dangerous structure due to that fire, so we'll just be shooting through the doorway. Nothing to worry about."

If Paul had felt uneasy in the Cotter's old apartment, standing in the entrance to the East Wing induced near panic. He struggled to respond coherently to questions and had to force himself not to keep glancing backward. He felt sure the shadows were gathering just out of his field of vision, forming into human-like shapes. He imagined darkness deepening in corners, preparing its assault.

This might be the time Palmer attacks, he thought. *The whole bunch of us in one confined space.*

Mia's customary buoyancy became frayed as Paul stumbled through his answers. Lucas, word perfect during his segments, regarded the American amateur with thinly concealed disdain. Joe emitted a few sighs as they reshot sequences again and again. Only Laura retained a sunny disposition, seemingly sympathetic to Paul, despite having to repeatedly 'go again'.

Eventually, Mia declared she had enough material.

"Okay, Joe, let's set up the motion cameras in all the key sites. Paul, if you want to come along, that's fine. If not, also fine."

As the cameraman and sound engineer checked their gear, Mia paused and sniffed the air. She turned to Paul.

"Can you smell something a bit—off? Like rotting meat?"

As soon as she mentioned the stink, Paul realized he had been smelling it for a while. His nervousness had distracted him. But now that he focused on it, it was very unpleasant.

"Maybe a dead animal?" Mia hazarded. "Perhaps a few wayward pigeons, or a stray cat, got trapped inside and died in the East Wing?"

"Another good reason to stay out of the place," Paul murmured, moving off down the corridor.

***

Joe Durham did not much like Rookwood. He had spent over twenty years in the business and had been working on Great British Hauntings for three. He hoped the show would continue to get decent ratings, as it was easy to make, and he had an ex-wife and daughter to support. Unlike a commercial, costume drama, or an artsy independent movie, Joe was not required to be too precise on GBH. In fact, the rough-edged, 'found footage' look was precisely what was needed. And until now, he had not been bothered by the idea of going into supposedly haunted places.

Joe did not believe in ghosts. He knew ninety-nine percent of the supposedly strange phenomena caught by himself and Laura could be explained very easily. That left one percent he could not explain, and he was happy to play along with Mia and act baffled by odd sounds or strange shadows. But Joe felt sure, if someone with more expertise looked at the 'ghosts' he had captured, they would find rational explanations.

But this is different, he thought, as he hefted the cases containing the motion-sensitive cameras. *This place feels wrong. The Yank has a point, even if he is a bit loopy.*

"Okay," said Mia, as they reached the first floor. "We'll set up the first inside the Cotter's flat. Which is—hang on, it's along here."

Mia turned left and set off along the passage, then hesitated. Joe stood watching her, puzzled. The entrance to the flat was opposite the stairwell, right in front of him. He pointed this out to Mia, who laughed and came back.

"Of course, it is. It's just these anonymous corridors are all the same. Whoever designs these places needs a personality transplant."

"Keeping costs down, I guess," Joe remarked, happy to chatter as they set up the device. He felt a need to keep Rookwood's silence at bay. There was something about the acoustics in the place that seemed to absorb sound, abolish echoes. He made a note to ask Laura if she had noticed it.

Site by site they moved through the building, staking out areas where supposed paranormal activity had occurred. Several times they got turned around, the bland anonymity of rooms and corridors proving deceptive. At least, that was what Mia blamed, and Joe was almost convinced.

But not quite, he thought. *There's something wrong here. The weird image I caught at the gate, that's hard to dismiss. Laura's analysis of that strange message looked spot on. And now this; two grown-ups getting confused in an empty apartment block.*

"Which floor are we on?" asked Mia with a frown.

"Second," he said. "This is Paul's old flat, isn't it?"

Mia looked puzzled for a moment, then laughed, slightly nervously.

"Course it is," she said. "You're right, they all look the same."

She sniffed the air again.

"Is it me, or is that stink wafting around up here as well?"

Joe concurred. The noxious smell had become more evident as they worked.

"The place has been abandoned for nearly a year," he pointed out. "Plenty of time for a dead rat or two to get really ripe."

Mia would normally have laughed at that, but she wrinkled her nose in disgust.

"Thanks for that image. Okay, let's deal with the East Wing, then we're done."

***

Paul opted to return to 'base camp' with Laura and Lucas. The actor, cursing his phone, promptly went outside to 'try and get a bloody signal'. Laura smiled knowingly and invited Paul to join her at the cluttered desk. The complex software she had used earlier was running.

"I've been looking at the background noise," Laura explained. "The low, erratic hum that almost drowned out your ghostly friend."

Paul watched as Laura went through a series of complex procedures using her fancy software. Her explanations of what she was doing were surprisingly clear. Firstly, she removed as much of the 'Liz signal' as she could. Then, she cleared up and boosted the background noise.

At first, Paul wondered why she was bothering, but then he saw the point. Like the original message, the sound that lurked behind and beneath it was more complex than it seemed at first. As Laura slowly worked her digital magic, they gradually heard an apparently wordless roar become something else. A single, male voice shouting to be heard over a chorus of howls, wails, bellows.

"Again," said the sound expert, "I can isolate a few syllables, gradually pick out words. If we're lucky. You can hear it's definitely a voice, anyway."

"Yes," said Paul. "And I know whose voice it is."

Laura looked up in surprise, smiled uncertainly as her mouse-hand hesitated.

"Another friendly ghost? No, I guess not from your expression. So, who is it?"

Paul leaned over to stare at the wavey form on the screen.

"Max Rodria," he said. "The scientist at Tynecastle U who thought he understood the nature of hauntings. Now he's become part of one."

Laura mouthed the word 'wow' as she resumed her task. At the next pass of her cleanup program, Rodria's words were almost comprehensible. What disturbed Paul more than the message, though, was the way the dead researcher sounded. Rodria in life had been an arrogant man with an orotund manner, always certain of his right to speak and be listened to. But now he sounded desperate, afraid, a soul in torment.

"He's crying out in the darkness," Paul whispered.

Laura glanced up, showing slight alarm, and clicked a few on-screen controls. Then she paused.

"You sure you want to hear this?"

Paul considered the question. The Rodria he had known had not wanted to help anyone but himself. Chances were that, in death, the scientist was still just as egotistical, and was simply yelling for help. But there was always the chance the dead scientist had something more useful to impart.

"Play it, please, Laura," he said quietly. "You've gone to all this trouble."

The mouse-click was followed by a distorted bellow.

"Set me free, Paul! Help me! Free me from this purgatory!"

Paul relaxed, oddly relieved Rodria had not changed that much. He wasn't interested in anyone else, just himself. But then it occurred to him, perhaps Rodria's self-centered nature might have prevented him from being wholly submerged in the Palmer entity. This, in turn, gave him another idea. He asked Laura if she would mind turning on the same mic she had used earlier.

"Sure," she said, with a puzzled smile. "What are you going to do?"

"I'm going to ask a dead professor for some advice," Paul replied, straight-faced.

Laura took a breath, exhaled an 'ooh-kaay', and set to work. After a few minutes, she pronounced herself satisfied with the setup and told Paul he could set his questions. She also started filming him with a small camera, giving him an apologetic shrug. Paul grimaced, but accepted she had a job to do.

"What do we need to do, Max?" Paul asked, speaking into Laura's shotgun microphone. "How do we help you? Tell us how to set you free!"

The sound engineer, again wearing her noise-canceling earphones, frowned in concentration.

The words were fragmentary, the background a chorus of screams, bellows, howls. Paul thought, with a shudder, of the victims of the first fire at Rookwood. Dozens of patients and inmates had died, and apparently been subsumed into Palmer's mighty ego. But Rodria, it seemed, was still struggling against subjugation.

"What's that first word? Decoy?" he asked. "The last one might be 'fall'?"

Laura shook her head. Paul knew he should defer to her judgment but felt impatient as she tweaked and tinkered. She put her hands to the headphones and listened, face intent, for what seemed like an age. Finally, she nodded and looked up at Paul with a grim expression.

"Destroy it all. That's what he's saying, I'm ninety percent certain. Destroy it all."

CHAPTER 5

"Impressive!" said Mia. "Well done, Laura. And you, too, Paul."

Paul looked around at the team, trying to find the right words. Lucas was mildly interested in his self-absorbed way. Joe seemed slightly annoyed at having to shoot yet another scene with Paul, who had not impressed him earlier. Laura and Mia were, as usual, full of enthusiasm.

"None of you seem to get it," he said, wearily. "Here's an actual dead guy, killed by Palmer, saying we should destroy the place. It's not just a good soundbite."

Mia shook her head in a rather exaggerated show of patience.

"It's okay, Paul," she said soothingly. "We're not staying here long. We only have to spend the night. That's always vital, people associate night-time with spooks."

Paul tried to explain that most of the incidents at Rookwood had happened by day, so far as he knew. But he could see the team was just going through their usual routine. Despite his best efforts, Mia saw this as another day at the office. Joe seemed a little unhappy but not inclined to protest. Lucas was keen to finish up and get paid. Only Laura showed some doubt.

"I've never recorded anything like this before," she said to Mia. "I'm not saying we're in danger, but it is—well, it's weird. Kind of eerie."

Mia seemed to muse on that for a moment. Then Lucas emitted a guffaw.

"Come on, people," he said, making full use of his trademark 'wood alcohol' voice. "We've done dozens of these shows, and the most dangerous thing that ever happened was when Joe fell on his arse in a muddy puddle."

The cameraman did not look pleased to be reminded of the incident, but the other team members smiled at the memory.

"And now," Lucas went on, "we're worrying about an old building where a few bad accidents have happened?"

Seeing Paul's expression, the actor held up a hand.

"I know, Paul, your experiences were traumatic. I don't doubt that. But we are professionals who have faced many unusual situations. And all it takes is a positive, can-do attitude. Like that exemplified by our estimable leader, Ms. Callan."

Mia gave a little bow to acknowledge the tribute.

"I second that, of course," she said. "But let's strike a compromise, Paul. If anything, anything at all, that you find remotely threatening takes place, you can leave and still receive your full fee. How about that?"

"It's not about the money—" Paul began, but Mia shook her head decisively.

"I know you didn't want us to do this," she said, "but here we are, and we've got a show to make. So far, it's gone well. Now we've set up the cameras and mics around the place, we don't have to go wandering up and down the hallways. We can just get a few mood shots outside and then wait."

"Or go to the pub first, and then wait," put in Lucas.

This prompted a discussion, and Paul found himself sidelined as Lucas and Joe argued strongly for 'having a swift pint' before nightfall. Mia insisted they remain to do more background shooting, with Lucas walking around the building, talking about its history. The light, she pointed out, was right.

Outside, everyone found their phones were not working. Joe suggested they were in a blind spot where the local cell tower was blocked in some way. Laura commented they were on top of a hill, about a hundred yards from a tony residential area. Mia insisted they get on with the job in hand, and shooting began. After Lucas had reeled off a few remarks about Rookwood's history, Mia asked Paul to record another brief interview.

"But we'll do it outside the East Wing," she added.

Paul's heart began to pound in his chest as the team moved off, camera and sound tracking Lucas as the actor strolled confidently forward. The East Wing was all too familiar. Paul noted plastic sheeting covered the doors and windows, and some scorch marks were evident on the brickwork.

The recording went reasonably well, but as before, Paul felt uncomfortable. His back was to Rookwood and his spine crawled as he wondered what might be observing him and the others. However, he held it together as Lucas recited his scripted questions about the hideous 'accident' during the attempted refurbishment.

"And I understand there was a message on the wall, in the poor chap's blood?"

Paul nodded, explained as best he could about the clue, his research into Rookwood, the findings about Miles Rugeley Palmer.

"And this undead doctor is now haunting the place, commanding some kind of legion of ghosts?"

The glibness of the question annoyed Paul, but he answered as soberly and coherently as he could.

"I believe the Palmer entity is a force, a being if you like, dominated by one overwhelming ego, but consisting of many souls, spirits, psychic energies—it's not a conventional ghost. It's far more dangerous, a kind of monster if you like."

"And that's a wrap," Mia said decisively. "Great stuff, Paul. Now, let's get some shots of the actual woods, just for background, stuff we can voice-over with spooky music."

***

Mike Bryson found himself in a long, boring faculty meeting. He doodled on a notepad while a colleague droned about budget cuts, student numbers, fees, publicity campaigns. PowerPoint slides glided by, each more forgettable than the last. Everything except teaching students was covered. He wondered how long he would be stuck in the stuffy room. Looking around the table, he identified two people who were as bored as he was. But there were another two who just loved meetings and always had 'something to add', over and over again. He began to wonder if he would get out before dark.

He discreetly checked his phone, tried to resend the message to Paul, outlining Percival's ideas. But, as before, it failed. Frowning, he speculated if sending a letter might be more effective. He also wondered if letting Paul know about Percival's 'god merger' theory would be of any use.

Can't hurt to drive up there after this bore-fest is over, he thought. *I could pop into that pub for a meal, maybe have a swift half.*

Mike suddenly became aware of the silence, faces turned toward him. He had obviously been asked a question. He looked up at PowerPoint guy and smiled.

"Sorry," he said. "I was just trying to warn a friend he might be in danger from a combination of a long-dead mad scientist and an ancient pagan god. So... I'm sorry, I completely forgot your name. What was it you asked?"

***

"Any weird stuff?"

Laura looked up at Paul from her laptop, smiled. The most approachable member of the TV crew, Laura had obligingly checked over her outdoor recordings. She shrugged, gestured at one audio file on the screen.

"I think I just got some local wildlife, that's all. Wanna hear it?"

Paul nodded, and Lisa clicked *Play.* The laptop speakers emitted a deep, booming note that sounded both sad and somehow ominous. It was just audible over birdsong and the traffic on the roads surrounding Rookwood's grounds. Laura played the file through a few times. Paul had no idea what the noise might be, but it sounded organic, not mechanical.

It was close to a roar, almost a parody of a Hollywood movie monster. But there was nothing remotely funny about it. As the file played through again and again, Paul felt his depression rising, like a black tide. The sound embodied loneliness, despair, and perhaps a kind of madness.

A living thing. Or a thing that was once alive? But it's not happy, that's for sure.

"What's that?" asked Mia, her voice unusually subdued.

Quietly, the rest of the team had gathered round. Laura played the brief clip again.

"Prize for the most plausible suggestion," she said perkily.

"Could be a horn from a passing truck, I suppose," Joe hazarded, but this idea won no support. Mia said something about freak atmospheric effects but was clearly baffled. To Paul's surprise, it was Lucas who seemed certain about the origin of the sound.

"That's a red deer. A stag," the actor declared. "They make a lot of noise in the mating season. They call it belling, short for bellowing I suppose."

"How do you know that?" asked Laura, genuinely impressed.

"When we were filming episode fifteen of Grist," Lucas began, to general sighs.

The anecdote took a while, but eventually, Lucas got to the point. During a location shoot on an English country estate, the noise of stags from a nearby forest had constantly interfered with sound recording.

"I'm sure that's a stag," the actor concluded. "Though, how one could have ended up in such a small clump of trees is beyond me."

Paul thought about Percival's idea of the nature god, always horned or antlered, a deity jealous of its domain. He decided against mentioning it, as he was sure any real threat must be from the Palmer entity and within Rookwood.

"Chalk that one up to unexplained," Mia declared. "Label the file

'Possible ghost stag' and move on, I guess."

At that moment, the other laptop pinged loudly. Joe, who had turned away from his computer, looked around in surprise.

"Bloody hell," he said. "We've got movement."

Joe's screen was divided into six rectangles, each one feeding live video from a different camera if motion sensors were tripped. He enlarged one feed to fill the screen. Paul could see it was from the camera they had positioned at the entrance to the East Wing. A shadow moved on the scorched walls of the room. Paul braced himself for the appearance of the Palmer entity in some form. He recalled a shadowy cluster of figures swiftly merging into one. But instead, something utterly unexpected lurched into view.

"Bloody hell, it's just some bloke," Joe exclaimed. "A trespasser, one of the local yobs."

"Should we call the police..." Laura began, then stopped. "Oh, right, the phones."

"Just go down to the gates," suggested Lucas. "Get that security guard fellow to leave his little kiosk."

Paul noticed wryly that the actor was not volunteering for the task, and was about to do so himself when Mia took charge.

"Just a minute," she said, looking more closely at the screen. "Let's see what this guy is doing first."

The figure, Paul saw, had it's back to the camera and was walking, slowly and stiffly, across the debris-strewn floor of the room. There was something odd about its posture. It was evidently male, and the clothing suggested a young person. But it moved like an arthritic pensioner.

"Might be hurt," opined Laura, as the mystery person lurched out of view. "Perhaps we should check?"

"Drugs," suggested Joe. "Something that turns them into zombies..."

He trailed off, realizing what he had said.

"Figuratively speaking," he finished lamely.

"Oh, come on," said Lucas. "You young chaps come with me, and we'll see what the little bugger is up to."

Joe stood up, looking uncomfortable, but obviously shamed into doing the 'manly' thing.

"Probably just a local thief trying to steal some copper wire," he grumbled. "Chances are he'll run off as soon as he hears us coming."

"Don't worry," Lucas said, "We can talk very loudly and give him plenty of warning."

Mia warned them to be careful and not take any risks. Joe picked up a lightweight camera and set off, followed by Lucas, with Paul bringing up the rear. Paul reflected, if a young criminal had broken in, it might give them a good reason to abandon the shoot. The thought made him feel slightly more enthusiastic, but he still stayed behind Lucas.

"Thing about criminals," the actor was saying, "is most are stupid opportunists with very little self-confidence."

My God, Paul thought. *He thinks having played a detective has made him an expert on lawbreakers. Let's hope it doesn't come to violence.*

"Is it me?" Joe asked, raising his voice a little, "or is that stink getting worse? Maybe it's a really ripe homeless guy."

They reached the automatic camera at the threshold of the East Wing. While the noxious smell was indeed much stronger, there was no sign of the mystery intruder. They moved cautiously into the room, and Joe crouched to get a better angle. The cameraman put one hand on the floor to steady himself, then recoiled in disgust.

"Oh, God. What did I put my hand in?"

As Joe focused on an oval patch of brownish fluid, Paul scanned the rest of the floor. He saw a line of similar patches leading past the fixed camera, out of the room, and into the corridor. He pointed this out to the others.

"Muddy footprints?" suggested Lucas.

"This is not regular mud," Joe grunted, wiping his fingers on his jeans. "And it stinks, like rotten meat."

There was a faint sound of movement echoing down the corridor. All three men froze and stared at the inner doorway. Then, still without speaking, they began to retreat to the entrance. Lucas, backing up clumsily, stumbled against the fixed camera and knocked it off its tripod. The accident prompted a volley of curses from Joe, followed by an argument, and for a moment, something like normality seemed to be restored.

Then Paul felt the temperature start to fall. The unnatural chill swept over him and he shuddered.

"Guys," he said urgently, but Lucas and Joe had already noticed.

"What's happening?" Joe asked, his breath clouding the air.

"Palmer's coming, we've got to get away," Paul said, trying to push by the other two. But the actor and cameraman were seemingly frozen in place. Then Paul realized they were gazing, eyes wide, at something behind him. He spun around and saw shadows growing, deepening, in the upper corners of the room.

"We should have stayed together, one group," he gabbled. "If Palmer takes over the most vulnerable person here, it will be harder for us to restrain him."

The other two looked at him vacantly, but he saw understanding start to dawn on Joe's face.

"Run!" he shouted, turning to flee. "Just get away, this is where Palmer's strongest!"

A moment later something struck Paul viciously across the shins and sent him sprawling. He landed heavily and tried to roll over. Lucas was standing over him with the camera stand, wielding the metal tripod like a bizarre club. Behind the actor, Joe dropped his own camera and lunged for Lucas, who fought back with startling ferocity.

Paul staggered upright and tried to help Joe restrain Lucas. The old actor fought fiercely, kicking and punching, even biting. But then, as suddenly as the attack had begun, it ended. Lucas became limp, his eyes rolled up into his head, and he slumped to the floor. Paul and Joe caught him before he struck his head on the tiles.

"What the hell was that?" Joe demanded.

"I can still see your breath," Paul pointed out. "Let's drag him out of here. You lift him under the shoulders, I'll get his legs—Joe?"

Joe was backing off down the corridor, eyes wide with panic. Paul spun around and saw a wall of darkness that almost blotted out the room beyond. It was the Palmer entity, stronger than ever before. And, Paul suddenly understood, it had what it wanted. With Lucas unconscious and Joe running away, Palmer could deal with Paul. The chill overwhelmed him, forced him to his knees, paralyzed him.

The darkness ebbed and flowed, tormented faces whirling in the icy cloud, then it condensed to become a squat, vaguely human-like figure. Two dim lights gleamed where eyes might have been. Paul remembered Palmer's old-fashioned, round-rimmed spectacles. For a moment, a fleeting thought tugged at his mind; the question as to why the glint of those glasses, of all things, should have endured.

And then he was simultaneously Paul Mahan and Miles Rugeley Palmer, experiencing the man's life, death, and post-death existence in one chaotic burst of sensory input. It was horrifying, and not just because of the things the man had done. Accessing Palmer's bloated ego revealed how utterly devoid of compassion and integrity the man was.

Even more confusingly, Paul was assailed by fragments of the personalities Palmer had absorbed and enslaved. Tormented souls, pale shadows of Palmer, orbited the doctor's vast, hungry ego. Cries of pain, despair, psychic wails, echoed through Paul's mind. Among the voices, he heard Max Rodria, still crying out for personal deliverance.

Then he had passed through this layer of lost souls and was truly 'inside' Palmer. The doctor's memories cascaded over him and, though he tried to resist, he found himself immersed in Palmer's personality.

CHAPTER 6

"What happened?" Mia demanded.

The two women had almost collided with Joe as he fled the East Wing. Mia had insisted he come back with them, shaming the cameraman into cooperation. Joe's account of what had happened seemed inadequate to the director.

But, she told herself, *these macho types are often the first to cave in.*

When they got to the connecting doorway, they found Lucas bending over Paul. The actor looked up, his expression frightened and concerned.

"I don't know what happened," Lucas said, his voice oddly hushed, lacking in confidence. "One minute we were—I just don't remember."

"Did he hit his head? Might he have a concussion?"

Mia fired off the questions but got no answer from either man.

"Joe, focus, did he fall?"

"Lucas attacked us," Joe said accusingly.

"I did not!" cried Lucas. "I had some sort of—blackout."

Laura had folded her jumper and put it under Paul's head. As she touched him, she pulled her hand back, shuddering.

"God, he's really cold!" she said, looking up at Mia in alarm. "We need some help."

Mia was already taking out her phone when she remembered the signal problem. Still, she decided it was worth a try. As before, though, no service was available.

"I got zero bars," said Laura, putting her own phone away.

"I'll run down to the gateway," Joe said. "That security guy must have a phone or a radio."

Without waiting for Mia's say-so, the cameraman ran back toward the foyer.

"Something spooked him," Laura said. "In the meantime, we'll have to try and keep him warm, I suppose."

Mia took off her own jacket and laid it over Paul. She put a hand on his forehead and pulled back in alarm. It was as if all heat had been drawn out of his body. And yet she could see him breathing. As she leaned closer, she saw the American's eyelids flicker.

"Is it hypothermia?" Laura asked in an awed voice. "He's so cold!"

"On a bright summer's day, in England?"

Mia shook her head.

"Looks like we've got solid evidence of the paranormal, right here."

She picked up Joe's discarded camera and started filming. Seeing Laura's expression, she snapped at the sound engineer.

"Yes, I know, but we can't do anything else that's useful."

Mia stood up to get a wider shot, then noticed Lucas standing by, looking on in evident confusion. The old man had a large bruise emerging on the side of his face. Mia swung the camera toward him.

"Lucas, were you hurt, too?" she asked.

"I suppose so," the actor replied. "But when it was happening, I don't think I felt anything."

"When what was happening?"

Lucas started to speak, stopped, tried to form words as she zoomed in on his face. The man who had been Inspector Grist suddenly looked very weary, as well as very muddled.

"It was as if—as if all the evil in this place ran through me, like a cold river," he said finally. "All the madness, all the cruelty. I was wrong to be skeptical."

Lucas was looking toward the camera, but his eyes did not seem to be focused on anything. She thought he was struggling to grasp an elusive, unpleasant memory.

"The spirit of this place—Mia, it's vile. And it's so powerful. We should get out!"

Mia put the camera down. She was unsure what was happening, only that it was dangerous.

"Right," she said. "We go together. Lucas, take his legs, we'll take his arms."

***

Within the Palmer entity, one man's life was lived over and over again, an obsessive reliving of personal history. It was a pocket universe controlled by an amoral narcissist.

Paul experienced what it was like to be a spoiled little English boy, son of an arrogant, domineering father who seemed to be perpetually disappointed by little Miles. Palmer's mother was a shadowy presence, almost permanently confined to her sickbed, dead before the boy's sixth birthday. A winter funeral and the sting of tears flashed by, a brief, poignant memory. Palmer recalled an elder brother, kind in a brisk, upper-class way, who went to a war that overshadowed his schooldays. It had been the 'war to end war', the Great War. The brother had not come back. Life became a little colder and darker.

Palmer, Paul discovered, had been small and timid as a child, inclined to live in a world of his own. His father, bereft of his favorite son, was now openly contemptuous of little Miles, the weakling, the 'runt'. Sent away to an expensive school for 'young gentlemen', he had been bullied. Paul experienced humiliation, the fierce shame of a child mocked and belittled. Palmer had retaliated not by making friends, but by snitching on more popular boys.

Paul also felt Palmer's keen intelligence growing, evolving, becoming obsessive. His interest in science had been his one real pleasure, but his cold, amoral nature had led him to cruel experimentation. Dissecting the headmaster's cat had proved the final straw, and Palmer was expelled. His father had given him a severe beating over that, but also hired private tutors to get him into medical school. Palmer had resolved to become a doctor.

The adult Palmer had been a plump, short, unimpressive figure. A winning personality might have canceled out these disadvantages, but Palmer was also arrogant, and girls found him laughable, sometimes downright repellent. Emotionally stunted and sexually frustrated, Palmer was driven by a burning resentment against the world, which he blamed for his own insignificance. In the new science of psychiatry, he sensed an opportunity to become wealthy and successful. After obtaining his degree, Palmer planned to set up as a psychotherapist for the rich and influential. Through them, he might achieve a great deal, without taking too much time and effort. His father refused to stump up the money. But Palmer senior was old and ill, his health undermined in part by grief at his older son's death.

I know what comes next, Paul thought. *I can feel his grubby mind working.*

Paul suddenly found himself in a room lit only by a coal fire crackling in a huge, old fashioned fireplace. A wizened, gray-haired man was slumped in an armchair. Paul felt a sense of triumph, and realized Palmer was watching his father die. The old man reached out, tried to speak. He was having a seizure. A bottle of pills on a small table was just out of reach. Knowing the servants were already in bed, Palmer left the room, planning to return the following morning after the body had been discovered. He did not bother to feign grief when he received 'the bad news'.

Paul was not surprised by the revelation, but his revulsion almost interrupted the connection with the Palmer entity. Intense moral outrage was, it seemed, something Palmer could not entirely accept. It was alien to his nature and caused him some confusion when it erupted so close to the core of his being. For a moment, Paul felt himself breaking free of the dark cloud, and tried to increase his disgust at Palmer's patricide. But he could not fake it. Fear and trepidation returned, and the cold grasp of Palmer reasserted itself. Once again, Paul was reliving the doctor's life.

Thanks to his inheritance, Palmer achieved his ambition. He

gained access to the British upper classes, and by the mid-Nineteen Thirties, was a well-known figure among London's elite. He made a point of pandering to rich men and women with minor or imaginary complaints, lending a sympathetic ear to the bored and self-indulgent.

He also supported British fascists. With repugnance, Paul saw how impressed Palmer had been by the ideology of Hitler. The doctor had imagined a future in which 'defective' and 'inferior' subjects could be experimented upon without legal restraint. Because, like many Nazis and Nazi sympathizers, he had developed a fixation with the paranormal. To demonstrate the proof of telepathy and other psychic powers would finally quench his burning ambition to be not merely admired and respected, but adored. He dreamed of his Nobel acceptance speech, honorary doctorates, lavish praise from kings and presidents. And the vulgar multitude? They would adore him.

To be worshipped, thought Paul. *That's what he wanted all along.*

***

Joe tried to wrench open the front doors, but they were too well secured. He toyed with breaking the glass, then thought better of it. Instead, he ran back to the storeroom and the only exit he knew to be unlocked.

Except it wasn't. Disbelief gave way to rising panic as he grappled with the handle, then slammed himself against the door. It shook but did not give way. He stepped back hastily, took a run, and shoulder-charged the door. He bounced off, agony shooting through his shoulder and upper arm, making him sob with pain and frustration. He remembered the toolkit he always carried, the screwdriver set. But it would take forever to remove the lock.

Joe returned to the idea of smashing one of the big glass doors in the foyer. He grabbed one of the folding chairs they had brought that morning and rushed to the inner door. But just before he reached it, the door slammed shut. Joe, aware he was losing it, could not help trying to bash his way out with the chair, reducing it to a few pieces of twisted metal.

The toolkit!

He went to his bag, got the screwdrivers out, and went to the outer door. Joe's hands were shaking as he selected the right tool. He stopped to take a breath, ordered himself to calm down. He thought of the outside world, sane and more or less orderly, just a few inches away on the other side of a slab of wood. The lock was nothing. He could do this.

Joe placed the head of the screwdriver carefully, gave it a firm twist. It slipped. The screw was firmly in place. He tried again.

***

"I can't do this!" exclaimed Lucas, dropping Paul's legs. They had only carried him a few yards up the corridor.

"For Christ's sake, man!" Mia shouted. "You've got to help!"

"Don't you understand?" the actor shouted, pushing past her. "We'll be next! Just leave him."

They shouted after him, trying to shame him into coming back, but he was deaf to their pleas. The two women watched as Lucas stumbled away, ranting about 'evil' that would 'claim them all'.

He's a bit of an old ham, Mia thought, *even when he's completely sincere.*

"What do we do now?" asked Laura.

Mia could see her colleague was close to panic, and desperate for some reassurance. She tried to think of something truly original and inspiring to say but failed.

"We'll be fine, Laura," she insisted. "Now, as to what we do—you take his legs, I'll lift him under the arms. He's not that heavy."

They lifted Paul as best they could and started to half-carry, half-drag the inert body down the hallway. She winced as heat drained from her fingers, as if they were carrying a statue carved from ice. The fierce cold, Mia realized, was not so much in Paul's body but surrounding it as a kind of aura. She thought of the American's descriptions of the Palmer entity, and how casually she had filed them away as a variation on so many stories of cold spots and strange presences.

Well, she thought, *now I've got proof of the paranormal that nobody can deny. All we have to do is live long enough to get it out there.*

***

Within the maelstrom of Palmer's bloated, twisted psyche, Paul continued to endure his captor's sordid, loveless memories.

The Second World War came and Palmer's fascist connections suddenly made him unpopular. He was drafted into the army, due to a lack of influential friends to keep him out of uniform. He proved a competent military doctor, and rehabilitated himself, pretending to repent of his extreme politics. Palmer despised ordinary medicine and saw his time in uniform as a period of necessary, if tedious, obscurity. Only one wartime moment burned bright, for monstrous reasons.

Palmer had entered one of the Nazi concentration camps in western Germany in 1945. He had supposedly been sent to help the starving survivors, but quickly allocated such mundane tasks to subordinates. He had instead set off to search the site for the medical block. Paul shared his excitement as Palmer opened the door to the operating theater, gave a perfunctory glance at surgical instruments and equipment, then started rifling through files. Then came disappointment, disgust, the realization that what he had hoped to find must be in the Russian-occupied part of Europe.

He had hoped he'd find the results of experiments on inmates, Paul realized. *But all he found was evidence of doctors doing their job.*

A few more images flashed by as Palmer re-established himself in post-war London. But his memory of the German camp stayed with him, frustration having planted a seed. Palmer wanted his own private laboratory, full of human guinea pigs. This ambition, combined with his enduring fixation with the occult, led him to Tynecastle, and the run-down, poorly managed Rookwood Asylum. It was the perfect choice.

Paul stood in Palmer's shoes in front of a committee of civic worthies, telling them just what they wanted to hear. It was easy to size up this bunch of unimaginative provincials, willing to be impressed by scientific jargon, and eager to be told not too much money would have to be spent on food or facilities for inmates.

"I will run Rookwood far more efficiently, using modern methods," said the doctor. "Insulin shock, electro-convulsive therapy, induced comas—these are all modern treatments that will calm down and possibly cure the most troublesome patients."

Paul felt Palmer's glow of self-satisfaction as the committee of worthy gentlemen commended his dedication and praised his excellent credentials. Now he had his own domain. At first, he was careful to follow official procedures, but in the nineteen fifties, these were lax enough to allow him broad discretion. Palmer selected what he considered to be promising subjects, the ones with the highest apparent intelligence, and attempted to discover their psychic abilities—if any.

He experimented with massive doses of insulin to induce comas in violent patients. He lobotomized other individuals to make them less troublesome. And, above all, he insisted on purchasing the newest electro-convulsive therapy machines. He became fascinated by the effects powerful shocks could have on the cerebral cortex, and the more secure he felt at Rookwood, the more experiments he undertook. Soon, he was combining powerful psychotropic drugs with ECT to try and induce ever more extreme mental states in patients.

The first significant result came with a huge, normally docile, individual known to the staff and other patients as Big Frank. The man had been admitted because of a violent outburst that left two policemen seriously injured. Big Frank had the mind of a child, and Palmer had little interest in a subject he viewed as mentally defective. Seeing him and several others as useful control subjects, Palmer tried him with the Zener cards.

Frank was strapped into a chair too small for him, the metal frame almost invisible under his huge body. The 'idiot' had been given a hefty dose of scopolamine before an ECT treatment. At first, Frank refused to cooperate, but a swift beating from one of the heftier attendants changed his simple mind. Palmer, Paul noted, felt distaste at the use of violence. This was not because of any squeamishness about inflicting pain and injury. It simply offended his sense of tidiness.

Palmer was disappointed to find that Frank did not seem to have any psychic ability. Tests with the Zener cards showed the 'defective' guessed the correct symbol at an average level. Palmer decided to keep Frank as a control subject, repeatedly testing him to ensure he had a good benchmark for the psychically talentless.

When another low IQ subject revealed some psychic talent, he was surprised and decided to expand the scope of his work. As his studies progressed, he revised his theories, concluding that intelligence and paranormal abilities were largely unrelated. He had previously confined his experiments to the brightest inmates of Rookwood. Now he felt justified in 'testing' every single one.

***

Lucas fled, ignoring the cries from the women behind him. Somewhere he felt shame. Inspector Grist would not have run out on 'damsels in distress'.

But you're not a hard-bitten detective, said a small voice. *You're just a washed-up actor.*

"I've got to get out!" he muttered. "Then I can get help."

It was a threadbare justification for leaving the others, but he felt the need to cling to some semblance of dignity. Lucas half-persuaded himself that he was not panicking, not simply running away.

He reached the end of the corridor and entered the foyer. The main doors were, of course, locked. He ran on, heading for the storeroom they called 'base camp', but slowed down. His initial terror had subsided and he was now feeling arthritic pain shooting through his knees. Every breath he took was painful, air rasping in his throat.

The door to the storeroom was locked. Lucas, almost bent double from his run, pounded on it with his fists. He heard a faint cry from inside, recognized Joe Durham's voice.

"Joe?" he gasped. "Let me—let me in!"

"I can't! Door's locked!"

Lucas staggered back, terror gripping him again. He was trapped in Rookwood Asylum, a place that had already possessed him once. He could not remember what he had done when under paranormal control, but he could still recall something evil worming its way into his mind. The thought it might do so again terrified him.

You could break out, said the small voice. *Grist would smash his way out, like a real hero.*

Lucas hurried back the way he had come, now feeling a growing pain in his left side, spreading across his chest. It occurred to him he might need medical attention as much as Paul. He passed a doorway marked MANAGER, stopped, on impulse tried the door. It opened, and inside the darkened office he saw a few random items of furniture. Among them was a standard office swivel chair.

"Ideal," he thought.

The chair had wheels, so he didn't need to carry it. He guided it clumsily out of the office, propelled it along to the foyer. He heard more shouting from the women but ignored them. Now, he was Grist, the competent man who could be relied upon in even the direst situation.

That's right, said the little, insinuating voice. *One big heave, and you're a hero again.*

Lucas wheeled the chair out into the foyer, achieving a kind of lumbering momentum. The chair crashed into the glass doors dead center and bounced off, jolting the actor badly. But he spotted a crack in one pane.

"Lucas! Stop!"

It was Mia's voice, seemingly calling to him from a very long way away. Lucas could barely hear her, or anything else, thanks to a booming sound in his ears. The foyer seemed to be getting darker, despite the clear view of sunlit lawn outside.

One more try. That's all it will take.

He pulled the chair back a few yards, tried another run up, but this time it seemed to have no effect. Frustration vied with pain and exhaustion, but behind them, all the driving force of fear endured.

Smash it like a man, the small voice urged. *You did your own stunts, do this one.*

Lucas bent at the knees and lifted the chair, trying to get it over his head. He flung it at the glass and noted with satisfaction that the damaged pane shattered into dozens of shards. Then it seemed as if his heart had burst, and a mocking voice spoke in his head again.

Well done! This was so much easier than controlling you directly. And much more fun.

Then he fell forward, through the hole, and the roaring blackness swallowed Inspector Grist and Lucas Sharpe forever.

***

If things had been bad before, Palmer's new policy made them far worse. Now every new admission was slated for ruthless, debilitating tests. The doctor's medical expertise was such that he never went too far. If an inmate had died it would have drawn too much attention. Palmer had the ability to push someone just far enough, exploit them fully, and then discard them, a still-living but almost mindless shell.

Palmer's prize subject finally arrived, the girl who was to prove his nemesis. Annie Elizabeth Semple was fifteen when she was impregnated, and her baby was taken from her shortly after it was born. Palmer barely noted the child was a girl. The point, for him, was simply that Annie Semple was considered unstable because she had not only committed adultery, but had done so while underage, and then been obsessed with keeping her illegitimate child. At seventeen, she was admitted to Rookwood, and quickly became what he called his 'star performer'.

Palmer forbade his staff from enjoying carnal pleasure with female inmates. This was not because of any moral concern, of course. He simply did not want any extraneous factors interfering with his experimental results. A mentally disturbed woman who had been raped might become even more erratic and uncooperative. Annie was younger and far more attractive than most of the female inmates, and so Palmer was especially rigorous in watching over her.

He saw himself as a kind of father-figure, Paul realized in horrified astonishment. *He assumed Annie would trust him, look up to him, be a dutiful little girl.*

Palmer's capacity for self-deception proved his undoing. Annie Semple was more powerful than any of his other subjects. But even Palmer underestimated her ability. His last experiment on her was also his last action as a living man.

Paul experienced the moments leading up to Palmer's death. Something like an earthquake had shaken Rookwood, causing panic among staff and inmates alike. Palmer's belief that Annie could become even more powerful had been demonstrated all too well.

Paul was looking out of Palmer's eyes as Annie, pale and unblinking, levitated toward him. Screams and shouts rang in his ears, and he felt Palmer lose control of his bladder. Big Frank grabbed him and dragged him back into the operating room where Annie had broken free. In his terror, Palmer realized his combination of drugs and ECT had somehow burned the fear from Annie's brain, liberating her powers and denying him any real control.

She lost her fear, he thought. *That was why she could defy him, before death and after. That's why Palmer was afraid of her.*

Palmer tried to protest as he was held down. Annie's psychokinetic powers fastened the restraints and put electrodes against his skull. Paul felt the cold metal, the pain as Palmer struggled against the over-tight straps, steel buckles cutting into his skin. Outside, the corridors echoed with screams of rage and panic, and the smell of burning was in the air. For a second, the doctor wondered if the power might fail, but it was a vain hope.

The amperage surged through his brain as he spasmed and writhed on the metal cot. Paul felt death closing, like a vast icy hand, on Palmer's mind. The doctor screamed in rage and panic, then bit through his tongue as another shock passed through his cortex. Blood filled his mouth. He spluttered and choked, pain from the wound conspiring with the agony of 'therapy' to almost blot out his consciousness.

Annie was sliding to the floor, blood streaming from her nose as her own much-abused brain finally gave way. Part of Palmer's mind was still sufficiently clinical to note her power was literally tearing her mind apart. Blood caked the front of her nightdress, but she smiled, nonetheless. She had her revenge. She nodded to Big Frank, who jerked the ECT machine's dial hard over, far into the blood-red of danger.

And then Palmer died, and Paul shared his death.

CHAPTER 7

"Oh God, I think he's dead!"

Laura looked up from Lucas' body, which lay halfway through the broken glass door. Mia saw the younger woman was close to complete panic and tried to think what to do next. She decided continuous action was the best way to stop Laura from dwelling on what had happened, and what might be about to happen.

"Look," she said quickly. "Joe's gone for help, so we can expect it soon. Let's get both these guys out of this place, okay? Starting with poor old Lucas. We can't be sure he's dead, we have a duty to try and help him."

Between them, they maneuvered the actor's inert body out of the glass door. Mia then kicked out the remainder of the glass with her boots, giving thanks she had opted for sturdy footwear. She was secretly half-convinced Lucas was dead, and that they were handling a corpse. But it did not bear thinking about, and she was not going to leave any member of her team behind if she could help it.

"Right, let's get him outside."

It was difficult to manhandle the actor through the shattered door, but they managed it. Mia looked out at the gates of Rookwood, hoping to see flashing lights, the distinctive livery of an ambulance. There was nothing passing by but regular traffic, however. A disturbing thought wormed its way into her mind.

Maybe Joe didn't make it.

She brushed the idea aside, urged Laura to follow her back in to retrieve Paul. But as she stooped to get through the smashed door, she sensed movement off to her right, in the corridor from the East Wing. At the same time, the foul stench that had assailed her nostrils earlier came back with vengeance.

The figure they had seen on the live video feed was shambling awkwardly toward her from the shadows. As it got nearer, the disgusting odor of rotten meat grew stronger, and Mia felt her stomach heave. Then she saw there was another shape moving behind the first, walking with the same jerky, spasmodic motion.

"Who—what do you want?" she shouted, trying not to let her fear show in her voice.

"What is it?" asked Laura.

"Get Paul," Mia urged, stooping to get a grip on the American. "Get him out."

Laura did not move, however. She stared at the approaching figures, then screamed. Mia had to look up and saw the first interloper had emerged into the light. It took her a moment to process what she was seeing.

The monstrous figure was dressed in bloodstained clothes and trendy runners that might be worn by any teenage boy. But it was hard to tell what the person had been from the state of their face. The flesh had partially fallen away from the bones, exposing teeth and skull. A brownish fluid trickled from the mouth and nostrils. The eye sockets were empty, yet the dead thing seemed to know where they were. It reached out its withered, rotting arms and fingers that were mostly bone covered with decayed cartilage.

Someone was screaming, and Mia realized it was not Laura. She reeled back, dropping Paul, thinking only of self-preservation. Laura was urging her to get out. The first animated corpse was almost within touching distance, and now she could hear the erratic squelching as its putrefying limbs drove it unsteadily toward her. Mia threw herself through the hole in the door, failing to roll successfully as she hit the gravel driveway, wrenching her shoulder. But the pain did not matter. As Laura helped her to her feet, all she could think was that the walking corpses on the other side of the doors could not follow her.

"Let's get to the gates," Laura urged, now sobbing with fear.

"Please, now, we can't do anything else!"

Mia did not reply, just set off down the driveway at a brisk jog.

***

Agony gave way to confusion, then rage as Palmer realized he was trapped in Rookwood. The catastrophic fire killed dozens of others, mostly inmates but also several male nurses and another doctor. All drifted through the corridors, lost souls bound to the scene of their deaths. Palmer reached out with his cold, precise mind, and began to conduct new experiments, unhindered by the obstacles of flesh. It took years of struggle, but Paul had already learned that time passed very differently for the dead. Eventually, all of the trapped beings at Rookwood were in Palmer's selfish orbit. All but one.

Annie Elizabeth Semple retained her power, and the fearlessness Palmer had inadvertently given her. She began to think of herself as Liz, no longer Annie the victim, but a brave new girl. As the Palmer entity evolved and grew stronger, though, Annie found it harder to resist and took to avoidance instead. Things were complicated by the fact that, if anyone died at Rookwood, Palmer could enslave them and thus become even stronger.

Seeing Liz from Palmer's viewpoint gave Paul a unique, disturbing perspective. To the monstrous entity the scientist had become, Liz was a wayward child who had defied her 'father'. She seemed tiny, weak, ignorant, yet at the same time dangerous in her potent psychic energies. It was the most twisted form of paternalism, Paul realized. Because he had given Liz her powers, Palmer saw himself as her creator. She owed him her loyalty, he felt sure. And, in return, he would absorb her into his psyche, thus completing the new, superior being he was trying to create.

The refusal of Liz to succumb was just one factor that had thwarted Palmer. The other was harder to define. At first, it had been a vague presence at the edge of the doctor's obsessive, focused intelligence. But recently, it had grown to become a disturbing third force, something that seemed to be gaining strength as the Palmer entity absorbed more victims.

Instability.

The third presence was something glimpsed, intuited, but never seen plainly and head on. It inspired fear, but also fascination. Paul, despite the suffocating power of Palmer's monstrous egotism, found he understood more about this presence than the insane scientist.

Cernunnos, Pan, Herne the Hunter. The Horned God, a nature spirit, a being with many names.

Palmer began to pick the knowledge from Paul's mind, part of the wider process of subsuming him into the great entity. Paul fought back as best he could, but Palmer was too strong. And he had another advantage—a psychiatrist's grasp of Paul's weakness. As well as fear and confusion, a familiar sense of despair began to close on Paul's mind. The dark tide of depression, the sense of utter powerlessness it brought, began to undermine his resistance.

***

Joe was on his knees. He had almost finished removing the lock from the outer door when he heard the inner door open. He looked around, hoping it was Lucas who had been hammering frantically for admission only a minute or two earlier. What entered, bringing a wave of chokingly foul air with it, was not Lucas.

As the first corpse stumbled into the room, it tripped, fell flat on its face, and thrashed decaying limbs. A hand came off, flopped heavily to the floor in a puddle of noxious fluid. The body began to crawl, lop-sided and slowly falling to bits, toward Joe. Beyond it, a second figure appeared in the doorway, its face glistening with rot. It stepped forward, moving like a marionette. But this one did not fall. Instead, it began to stalk clumsily across the room toward him.

"Oh God," whimpered Joe, turning back to the lock, twisting the screwdriver desperately. "Oh God, no."

He undid the last screw and pulled at the lock, then threw himself at the door. It still resisted, and he began to beat the wood panels in desperation. For the first time, he wondered if the door had ever been locked, in the conventional sense. Bony fingers grabbed at his ankles, clawed his back, found their way to his throat. Joe turned, screwdriver raised like a dagger, and began to fight for his life.

***

Mike Bryson pulled onto Blaydon Avenue and slowed down, looking for a parking space. As the gates of Rookwood came into view, he saw what looked like an altercation of some kind. Passing by, he saw Mia Callan and another woman, both apparently shouting at a confused security guard.

Not good, Mike thought.

He parked in the first spot he could find, then ran back along the road to the gateway. The security guard was now talking loudly into a walkie-talkie. Mike caught the word 'emergency', then 'at least two injured'. He quickly introduced himself and gathered Paul was in danger. He could tell from Mia's expression there was a lot more to it, but he could not simply stand by.

"You coming then, mate?" he asked the guard.

The man hesitated, and Mike pushed past, set off up the drive at a run. Behind him, he heard Mia shout a warning, but could not make out the words. As he approached the entrance to the apartment complex, he observed a smashed door and a body lying by the side of the pathway. His mouth grew dry as he approached, then saw the man was far older than Paul. He caught sight of his friend inside the foyer, his body sprawled like a rag doll.

Without hesitating, Mike climbed through the broken pane and knelt down beside Paul. A foul reek made him wrinkle his nose, and he noticed dark patches on the carpeting. But there was no sign of any danger. He reached out to try and take Paul's pulse, then jerked his hand back.

"Bloody hell."

For a moment, he thought he had somehow been burned, then realized it was an icy cold that had startled him. He forced himself to check the pulse in Paul's throat, found it was racing. Mike saw his friend's eyelids flickering and heard a faint moan.

No ordinary nightmare, I reckon, he thought, slapping Paul on the side of the face.

"Wake up, you lazy bugger!"

It didn't work, so he lifted Paul and dragged him toward the door. He saw no one outside, just the old man, who was quite possibly dead. The cold aura surrounding Paul seemed to be eating into Mike's bones, growing stronger. He felt his hands lose all feeling and had to let go.

***

You are nothing, the Palmer entity insisted. *There is no purpose or meaning to your life, or to anything else. Why resist? Why not yield to the darkness in the world? In the end, it always wins.*

The nihilistic force of Palmer's mind combined with Paul's depression to overwhelm him. Nothing mattered. He looked back over his life and saw a bleak and lonely emotional landscape, a career that had run into the sand, relationships that never went anywhere.

Nobody cares about you. Palmer's voice, precise and emotionless, echoed until it seemed to fill the cosmos. *You are nothing, no one. Surrender to reality, to the truth of oblivion. It all ends in death.*

Paul fought back, despite his almost overwhelming despair. He thought of Mike, who at that moment somehow seemed very close. Mike, the friend who genuinely cared, and never judged. He thought about Ella, the innocent child whom he wanted to help. He thought of his mother, his sisters, people who had loved him when he was young.

But your mother died in a madhouse, Paul. And where do you think you will end up if you survive this?

Paul felt the cold tide of despair rising, threatening to draw him under, strong currents of misery and sorrow pulling at his fragile selfhood. Soon he would be gone, no matter how hard he fought, just another slave to Palmer's overbearing egotism. But then, just as he was about to surrender, another voice sounded, barely perceptible but still familiar.

"Paul, don't give in!"

It was Liz, and in his mind's eye, he could see her shining faintly, a colorless light flickering against a vast darkness. The light grew brighter, but still seemed hesitant, and Paul thought of a ship battling through a storm.

"Liz?" he said, or tried to.

"Fight back! I'll try to help!"

Paul struggled to reach out to Liz, clutching at the faint, flickering light in the dark turmoil of Palmer's cruel universe. He tried to preserve his sense of self, prevent his identity from being eroded by the vicious countercurrents of Palmer's ravenous ego. Around him circled other souls; Palmer's victims, a few accumulated down the years, but mostly the dead from the fire in 1955. He saw faces contorted with fear, some choking, and realized most had died from smoke inhalation. A few, it was apparent from their scorched flesh, had burned. The dead closed in, their howling visages almost filling Paul's world, then all merging to become Palmer's smug, bespectacled face.

"Keep trying Paul! He isn't as strong as he seems!"

Liz's words were just perceptible, battling against the psychic tempest. What could she mean? But then Paul grasped her point. Most of Palmer's slaves, most of the subordinate beings that made up the larger entity, were insane, damaged, frightened, enraged. There were a few cowed doctors and other asylum staff, but they were outnumbered by the deranged dead, perpetually haunting the scene of their collective demise. Palmer had to exert a vast amount of his energy to keep them in line, to prevent his subjects breaking this evil gestalt apart. His unwilling subjects were hard work.

"That's why he wants you, Paul. That's why he wants the cleverer ones, the saner ones."

At that moment, Paul thought he understood the paradox of the Palmer entity. It was, in itself, a kind of asylum. It remained a more-or-less coherent whole so long as Palmer could rule his slaves through fear, constantly re-running their torment at his hands. In the case of Liz, it had failed—she had proved too wayward, too strong. Others, such as Rodria, were borderline cases, still struggling to escape. To stabilize itself the entity needed more rational, intelligent components, but ones who lacked confidence, who were too weak to challenge Palmer.

It needs people like me, he thought. *Someone smart enough to be useful, but not brave enough to fight him.*

The colorless light flickered, faded, and brightened again. It seemed to be getting closer, forging a path through the howling storm.

"Show him he's wrong, Paul!" urged Liz.

Paul tried to focus all his efforts on defying Palmer. He visualized smashing the dead doctor's self-image, imagined Palmer as a fat, ugly dwarf with ludicrous, pebble-thick spectacles. It was a cartoon version of the doctor, a satire on the little man who thought so much of himself.

Silly old fool! Paul thought. *Stuck in your derelict building, lording it over dead lunatics. A head full of fantasies, picking off the odd victim like any common murderer. You're pathetic! You're a freak, just a rogue byproduct of some ancient, psychic force.*

The reaction was immediate and furious. Palmer's round, glistening face grew, filling the dark sky, almost blotting out the glow that was Liz. As the face expanded, it also changed, the flabby extremities becoming more strongly defined, the spectacles vanishing, the snub nose growing aquiline. Palmer was exerting a tremendous effort to reshape himself into the heroic figure he had always wanted to be. Paul thought he recognized hints of Rod Taylor, Laurence Olivier, and other old-time actors in the face that formed in the nightmare sky.

But it did not quite work. The plump features of the short, round-shouldered psychiatrist kept reasserting themselves. Palmer could not quite banish reality, no matter how hard he tried. And reality conflicted with his splendid image of himself. Paul felt the frustration of the long-dead Palmer, and again the doctor's mental pressure bore him down, tried to absorb him.

"Paul? Can you hear me?"

The new voice was familiar, but it took him a moment to recall who was speaking. It was Mike Bryson, the prosaic, good-natured friend he had relied on so much. Again, he got the impression that Mike was close by, trying to help. Liz definitely seemed closer, now.

"Wake up, Paul!"

A surge of optimism allowed Paul to defy Palmer for a precious moment, and the vast face of Palmer started to disintegrate, dissolving into the surrounding chaos. Paul strove to wake up, to simply open his eyes and shake off the influence of the Palmer entity. He almost managed it. But then the next attack came. The entity channeled all its brute energy straight at Paul, not caring if he was harmed, perhaps even destroyed. All pretense at subtlety was abandoned.

Instead of waking up, Paul felt himself begin to weaken.

***

Mike slapped Paul on the side of the face, still feeling the sting of the intense cold that somehow wrapped his friend in a layer of icy air. The first slap didn't work, nor did the next three or four, each harder than the last. Mike felt angry at himself, having no idea what to do next. He wondered if whatever had attacked and terrorized the others would appear again, perhaps kill him. Or would the Palmer entity seek to possess him as it had evidently possessed Paul? Panic began to rise, and he looked out of the smashed door to see if an ambulance was appearing, or perhaps the police; anyone to take responsibility, to do something competent and save the day.

He saw nothing. His panic-fright continued to increase, so much so that his hands were shaking. This was more than stress, he felt sure. He looked around wildly, sure he was being watched. A shadow fell across the foyer, blotting out the summer sunlight. But when he spun around, he could not see anything.

Mike thought about the reason he had come here, Percival's theory that the ancient god might still be present. He recalled what the old man had said about such deities, the fear they inspired.

Pan, from which we get the word panic.

"Well," he said, loudly. "If you are there, you might do us all a favor."

"What's going on?" asked a deep voice.

Mike jumped up, backed against the broken door, almost fell through it. A bald, middle-aged man was standing, staring at him, panting heavily. The man held a screwdriver that seemed to be covered in blood and some revolting brown goop. His face was badly scratched down one side. There was a sudden stench in the foyer, a vile odor of rotting meat. Mike gagged.

"Sorry about the pong," the other man said. "I had this tussle with the undead."

"Who—what?" Mike struggled to find words.

"Never mind," said the stranger. "Call me Joe. What's been happening?"

When it became clear Mike knew very little, Joe nodded briskly.

"We need to get him out of the asylum," Joe said, bending over Paul, then pulling back one hand with a pained hiss.

"You were right about the cold," he admitted. "But maybe we can wrap our hands in something?"

Now that he was no longer alone, Mike felt some confidence returning. Joe, despite the foul odor he brought, seemed like a good bloke, someone who'd stand by you in a crisis. He took off his old sweatshirt and tore it roughly into four pieces, handed two sections to Joe, then wound the other two sections around his own hands for protection.

"Yep," he said. "Let's get going."

***

Just as Paul felt himself going under, unable to resist any more, a kind of miracle happened. The horrendous maelstrom of psychic energy seemed to weaken, and he felt Palmer show uncertainty. Paul heard voices, recognized those of Mike and Joe. The gleam that was Liz became stronger, while the monstrous ego of Palmer seemed to lose focus.

"Careful with his head."

It was Joe again. At the same moment, Paul felt the piercing cold start to yield. The nightmare vision of Palmer's inner world began to vanish. A reddish glow appeared, banishing the darkness. Bright sunlight was shining on his eyelids, he knew. He tried to open his eyes, look at the sane, human world, but could not.

Instead, he felt another presence invade his mind.

Paul was in a bright forest glade, looking down on what he thought at first must be a semi-circle of kneeling children. But no, the white-robed figures before him were full-grown men. He towered above them. Paul realized he was one with the nameless deity of the forest and had dwelt in Rookwood for thousands of years. He was real because of the earth-energy that focused on this point, and because the believers gave him shape and consciousness. He could no more leave the forest than he could leave the earth.

The worshippers placed offerings of meat, fruit, and some gold coins on a small stone altar before him, then fled Rookwood. He had no need for the things they left, but it was sufficient that they were precious to his followers. They made sacrifices so he would bless their hunting and their harvest. And he could do these wonderful things. In this small domain, he could control events with powers rather like those of the Palmer entity.

Then came a new religion. At first, it manifested itself as a few wooden churches, a new set of rituals. The cult of Rookwood existed alongside that of Jesus, the peasantry observing the old ceremonies in spring, summer, and autumn, just as they observed Easter and Christmas. But slowly, the deity felt its domain grow more cramped, its powers weakening.

People were losing faith in the old gods.

The scene changed, and there was fury and pain. Fury because the forest of Rookwood, after so many centuries, was finally being cut back, reduced to a mere fringe of trees. Each blow of the ax was agony for a being whose essence was interwoven with all the life of Rookwood. The nature god fought back but failed. In place of the trees and flowers and wild creatures, an ugly square-built structure was raised in brick and glass and stone. The deity of the forest could no more enter such a place than it could fly to the moon. It raged impotently and felt its power slip away. Its cries of anger turned to a forlorn lament, audible to few, then to none.

But one night, something strange occurred. It was so bizarre that even the forgotten god was surprised. The ugly block of brick and stone and glass burned, and there were cries of terror, flashes of unnatural light. Paul recognized the East Wing as it had been, on the night when Annie Semple had finally overcome her tormentor. Then he saw something else.

A new being, a rival god. A monstrous hybrid thing. A clump of deformed souls in thrall to a tyrant.

The forest deity, weak and confused, observed the rise of the Palmer entity with baffled resentment. The nature spirit could only look on as decades passed and more human souls were absorbed by the interloper. Soon, the old god of Rookwood sensed the entity wanted to break away, leave the ancient sacred site, and impose its will on the wider world. But it could not. As a god of madness, it seemed limited by the confines of the asylum building, just as the forest god was limited to the woodland.

Years passed, and it appeared both deities might gradually fade away. But then came more activity, and the old god looked on, impotent, as the asylum became a place for people to live. Some, the deity knew, would become sacrifices to the upstart rival. And, as the Palmer entity grew stronger, it would bleed away more precious energy from the sacred place, reducing the old god to a fading shadow.

Faced with oblivion, the nature spirit decided to fight back. It was not accustomed to struggling with other deities. It was, however, used to manipulating the minds of mortals. And now it reached into Paul, searching for a way to battle against the Palmer entity, puzzled by what it found. The modern world was almost incomprehensible to the ancient entity. But its presence, Paul sensed, was causing problems for Palmer. At the very least, the older god of Rookwood was distracting the would-be usurper.

"Fight him! Fight him now!"

Liz's urging spurred Paul on to more effort. As he battled to break free of Palmer's bleak universe, he felt Liz's presence nearby. A glimpse of her face, dark-eyed, still startlingly young, swam into his view. She smiled encouragingly.

"You can beat him, Paul. Don't let him take you!"

***

As Mike and Joe manhandled Paul through the smashed front door, the vicious cold seemed to lift. Mike could no longer see his breath in the summer sunlight. They were laying Paul down on the turf by Lucas Sharpe when the ambulance arrived, followed by a police car. At the same time, Mike saw Mia Callan and her colleague running up the driveway. He felt slight resentment at them deciding to return now.

After we did the heavy lifting, quite literally.

"He's not so cold now," Joe remarked, laying a bare hand on Paul's forehead. "Whatever it was seems to have—stopped, gone away, or eased off at least."

Mike stood up, gave a wave to the approaching vehicles, as if they needed guiding in. He immediately felt stupid, turned back to look into Rookwood, and felt his heart pause. Looking out through the smashed glass doors was a young woman in a gray dress, her hair unfashionably bobbed. Her dark eyes seemed to bore into him. She smiled, her surprisingly sensuous mouth twisting up at the ends. It was not a reassuring smile. Behind her, darkness swirled. For a moment, Mike thought he saw another figure, small and plump, a bald man wearing glasses. Then the reflection of the ambulance appeared, its whiteness sweeping aside the disturbing vision.

CHAPTER 8

"Lucas Sharpe had a heart condition. Undiagnosed, it seems, but quite serious."

Paul looked at the other man, could think of no reply. He was sitting opposite Detective Sergeant Farson. A microphone linked to an old-style cassette recorder was placed on a fixed-down table between them. The officer was dressed neatly in a short-sleeved white shirt, regulation dark tie, his face clean-shaven and almost unlined. It occurred to Paul that Farson must be around his age. He glanced past the detective at his reflection in the two-way glass of the interview room. Paul thought he looked about ten years older than Farson, maybe fifteen.

"He also had other health issues—drink, stress. Because he was in such poor shape, death is not being treated as suspicious, despite— some slight anomalies in the coroner's report."

Paul nodded, again unable to think of a response. He could hardly say the old actor had been possessed by the collective madness and rage of the old asylum, the psychic power marshaled by a long-dead psychiatrist with a god-complex. He had already given an official statement to the effect that Sharpe had 'gone crazy' and run away from Joe and himself. The police concluded the actor had died from over-exertion, trying to get out of a building that Sharpe had convinced himself was haunted.

"Then there are the corpses of those two teenagers," Farson went on, shuffling files on the tabletop. "Dead bodies, dead for several weeks, in fact—which your friend Joe Durham claims attacked him. You didn't see any of that?"

For a moment, Paul wanted to help Joe, offer some support to the cameraman. But he knew it would be futile, given his own record of mental health issues. He glanced at the mirror again, wondered who—if anybody—was watching. The police would presumably have a duty psychiatrist standing by for occasions like this.

"No," he said slowly. "We all detected a foul smell, like rotting meat, so the bodies were clearly in the building. But I didn't see them. I certainly didn't see them move. Except—"

"Except what?" Farson asked quietly, his level gaze unblinking. "Please don't omit any details that may help with this investigation, Paul."

Paul hesitated, wondering if the video shot by the motion-sensor camera would count for anything. All it really showed was a person who didn't belong to the TV team. Seeing Farson's expression, Paul knew the officer would not let the point drop. He explained a stranger had been caught on film. If Farson wanted to go chasing that elusive individual, good luck to him.

"Yes," Farson said calmly, "we have been reviewing files recorded by Mr. Durham and Ms. Blaine. Also, there's some phone footage from Ms. Callan. All trustworthy individuals, would you say?"

"Compared to whom?" Paul shot back. "Come on, you cops all know how unreliable witnesses tend to be, it's part of your basic training. You also know the more extreme the situation, the less you can trust people's recollections. And this was a very extreme situation."

Farson picked up a pen and made a note on a pad in front of him.

"True enough," he said. "And we appreciate your talking to us now. According to the medical report, you were found unconscious, having been carried out of the building by Mr. Durham and Mr. Bryson. Do you recall any events leading up to your—accident?"

Paul shook his head. His first real-world recollection after being attacked by the Palmer entity was waking up in the ambulance on the way to the Royal Victoria Infirmary in Tynecastle. When he arrived, he had been diagnosed with shock and, to the bafflement of the ER doctor, a touch of frostbite. Another anomaly that would be quietly forgotten, he assumed.

"Mr. Sharpe was still quite famous," Farson said, a remark that took Paul by surprise. But, when he considered the point, he appreciated the detective's words. The survivors of the latest 'incident' at Rookwood would be of even more interest to the media, mainstream and otherwise.

"You mean I should get out of town, or hide somewhere?" Paul asked.

Farson shrugged.

"What with the mysterious death of 'Inspector Grist', you can't blame people for being interested," he said in a neutral voice. "This is the second year running that deaths at Rookwood have made headlines. The point is, we can't really protect you from media attention. You'll just have to wait for it all to blow over."

Farson paused, then added, "There are a dozen reporters outside right now, pestering people wanting to report their neighbors' noisy parties."

Paul looked at his reflection again, saw a haggard, unshaven face. He began to imagine headlines about the American with 'issues' who had been present at the death of 'TV's much-loved Inspector Grist'.

"Your friend Mike is waiting at the rear exit," Farson said, smiling. "We're not monsters, after all. If you'll come with me, I'll show you out—this place is a bit of a labyrinth."

"Has anybody ever died in this room?" Paul asked, as Farson opened the door.

The detective looked surprised. His professional composure was ruffled for the first time since Paul had met him.

"Not that I know of," Farson said, after a short pause. "Why do you ask?"

Paul glanced at the figure hunched in the corner, clutching his knees to his chest, hollow-eyed and afraid. He had been trying to ignore the ghost, but the dead man's expression was too pitiful. There were bruises on the forehead, dark blood on the lower lip. Judging from the man's clothes, he had passed at least thirty years ago, maybe more.

"Nothing," Paul said, smiling briefly. "Just got a chill down my spine, is all."

***

"Is she okay?" Paul asked. "I didn't see any marks on her arms."

"She certainly seems to be enjoying herself," observed Mike.

They were sitting in the park with Neve Cotter, watching Ella feeding ducks. The girl was doling out proper bird feed, having informed Mike 'you should never give them bread, it's bad for them.' Mike had sheepishly binned the half-sandwich he had been about to throw to a mallard.

"She's been fine for a while, now," Neve confirmed. "Maybe this time she's finally free of it. Of Liz, rather. But I'm not counting my chickens."

Ella certainly seemed content and self-possessed to Paul. Neve seemed less stressed and had even laughed at some of Mike's attempts at humor. So far Neve had seen no evidence of Liz interfering with her daughter's life. It was a week since the chaos at Rookwood. Paul was cautiously optimistic, but still felt uncomfortable. He had been unable to convey to anyone the essence of what he had experienced at the former asylum. He had told Mike that Palmer had tried and failed to possess him, which was a half-truth.

"So, what really happened?" Neve asked, startling Paul. "Just idle curiosity, but how did you survive?"

"I think it was partly down to dumb luck," Paul admitted. "If Mike hadn't turned up when he did. If Joe, a guy I'd just met, hadn't been such a tough cookie. If Liz hadn't been on my side against Palmer. Whole lot of ifs. If I hadn't been lucky, I'd be gone."

There was a pause, and they continued to watch Ella rationing out her bird food to an ever-growing group of eager ducks.

"What about this bargain with Liz?" Neve asked. "You were

supposed to help her in return. But what can you really do?"

Paul shrugged. He felt uncomfortable, now, as he could not tell the whole truth. Instead, he dodged the question, arguing that more research into Rookwood might reveal a way to deal with the Palmer entity. He hoped he sounded convincing, but later—as they made their way back to the Cotter's home—he caught Neve looking at him. Her expression was hard to read, but he sensed doubt, uncertainty.

And she's right, he thought. *Because I know exactly what I should do.*

***

That night Paul woke in the small hours to hear sirens and saw the brief flash of lights as a police car or ambulance raced past the end of the street. He still panicked at loud noises, sudden shocks, raised voices. It was ironic, he felt, that the antics of the living should alarm him, when it was the onslaught of the dead that had nearly destroyed him.

He got up, rubbing sleep from his eyes, and went to look out the window. Sometimes he glimpsed ghosts by night, but this time there was nobody in sight. The only living creature was a black cat, slinking its way between and under parked cars. As the cat vanished, Paul wondered for the first time if animals, too, had ghosts. It seemed improbable. He made his way to the bathroom, on the way pondering whether sentience, self-awareness, was necessary for some kind of survival of a being after death.

Paul clicked on the bathroom light, and Liz looked up at him. She was standing just inches away, the familiar chill starting to draw heat from his body. He reeled back, almost fell through the doorway. Liz smiled, and Paul felt chill fingers grasp his arms, draw him back upright. Then he was urged gently into the bathroom and the door swung shut behind him. It was a reminder of her power and hinted what was to come would not be a negotiation.

"What—what are you doing here?" he asked.

Liz shimmered, grew transparent, then suddenly her gray-clad figure was even closer, her arms draped on his shoulders. Without thinking, he tried to push her away, but found he could not move his arms. The cold was much more intense, now, and becoming painful.

"I need you to fulfill your side of the bargain," she said. "I need you to do what has to be done."

He shook his head but could not bring himself to say 'no' to her. Looking into her big, dark eyes, he could not see his reflection. He was not there. All he saw was darkness, a lightless void he felt himself falling into.

"There must be another way," he said, his breath clouding the air between them. "I can't go back to that place. You know what will happen if I do."

This time Liz shook her head and smiled slightly. She stepped back, and the piercing coldness diminished a little.

"I understand you're afraid of him," she whispered. "But there is no alternative. You must go back and destroy it. Remember what Rodria said. Remember what we all said."

He tried to retreat, groping for the door handle, but when he touched the metal, it was so viciously cold he jerked his hand away, wondering if he left some skin behind.

"Give me time," he pleaded. "Just a little more time."

The light flickered and Liz was gone. He heard her voice, echoing faintly, as the temperature in the bathroom began to rise again.

"Don't delay too long, Paul. I'll be waiting."

Paul went to the sink, poured a glass of water, and took a gulp to ease his dry throat. He had goosebumps and walked quickly back to bed. As he passed Mike's room, he heard his friend snoring gently. He felt a momentary urge to wake Mike, share everything with him in a thoroughly un-British way. Then he thought better of it.

The less I involve people I care about, the better.

***

Two months passed. During that time Paul was granted leave from the university on condition he resumed therapy. He had been diagnosed with post-traumatic stress disorder, and his employers were keen to show they were doing everything they could for him. Paul suspected they would have gotten rid of him if they could, but as he had committed no crime, that was not an option.

Doctor Blume was, apparently, seeking help herself, so a new therapist was assigned. This one was brisk, rational, upbeat. It was easy for Paul to fake the right responses. Oh yes, he was feeling better. He was slowly coming to terms with his 'delusions'. The doctor was interested in results, and Paul contrived to deliver them. He talked with complete honesty about what he had experienced at Rookwood, and then accepted the therapist's rationalizations.

Paul avoided the press, complained to the British media regulator that his privacy was being invaded at a difficult time. Reporters backed off. They were not lacking in material, Paul noted, when Mia Callan and her team were so willing to give interviews. The TV crew played up all the weird and baffling aspects of the incident and released some video and audio material online. This led to the usual, ultimately futile arguments, as to how authentic any of their footage was. Then, inevitably, interest began to wane.

Paul remained in touch with Mia by phone and Skype. She told him she was planning a feature-length episode of her show, 'dedicated to Lucas, of course.' In fact, though she chose her words carefully, she had in mind a 'tribute' that would effectively cash in on the old actor's death. But to finish it, she wanted to talk to Paul. He dodged around the issue for a while, but finally agreed to meet up with Mia and the rest of the survivors at a remote house up the coast in Northumberland, not far from the Scottish border.

110

As well as Mike, Paul insisted on bringing an 'expert guest'. Mia was dubious at first, but when she met Lance Percival, Paul saw her eyes light up with enthusiasm. He had already warned the old academic he might be offered a guest spot on the show, maybe regular appearances.

Well, Paul thought, *there have been less likely partnerships in showbiz.*

The group settled down to discuss possibilities. Mia and her diminished team naturally focused on completing their show. But Paul, Mike, and Percival wanted to discuss the nuts and bolts of what had occurred. Paul tried to steer the conversation toward the only thing that mattered to him—how to get rid of the Palmer entity. After some initial irritation, Mia got Laura and Joe to start filming the discussion for filler material, or maybe a DVD extra.

"I think," said Percival, as Joe focused a lightweight camera on him, "the more living, human involvement the entity gets, the stronger it becomes. Remember, it was dormant for decades. I would argue that, like the nature god it usurped, the Palmer entity requires a form of worship to remain strong."

"Worship?" asked Mia. "It seems to just want to terrorize and kill."

"Precisely," responded Percival. "In modern terms, particularly those of a sociopath like Palmer, fear and death are ideal methods of achieving fame. The man's name is all over the internet, and people are routinely turned away from the gates. There are rival theories about it, most of them hokum of course, but the point is the attention of thousands, perhaps millions, is now focused on Rookwood."

Paul had already heard this theory, and it filled him with despair. If Percival was right, the public's endless appetite for violence and the paranormal would keep the entity strong. He had hoped leaving Rookwood alone might weaken the Palmer entity, make it less able to strike back at him. He put forward the idea now.

"Doesn't Palmer's need for more—hell, let's call them souls—doesn't that prove he needs more than attention? If he's deprived of more recruits, won't he lose power over time?"

Percival gave a wise nod, smiled as he put his teacup down and then tented his fingers in contemplation.

"I'm sure he would fade away—over historical time," said the old academic. "A forgotten god loses its power. But in what one might call personal time, the human lifetime, I believe Palmer will remain powerful for a good while, and probably absorb more unwary souls, unless something or someone stops him. He is not, after all, some old-time pagan deity. This entity was created in part by scientific thought, experimentation, and a very modern desire for notoriety. And he has grown in strength considerably in recent months."

"What could stop him?" Mia put in. "An exorcism, something like that?"

Percival shook his head decisively, while continuing to examine the plates of biscuits on offer. Eventually, he selected a Bourbon cream and used it to gesture emphatically.

"No traditional exorcism is likely to work," said Percival. "Firstly, it's a lot of superstitious folderol. Palmer, ironically enough, seems to have been an atheist, and we know he has no respect for the clergy. Secondly, even if some kind of ritual could be devised, a human being would have to be there to perform it, giving the entity just what it wants. No, I'm afraid nothing resembling magic or religion can succeed here."

"Then what about science?" asked Mike. "We seem to keep hedging around this point, but there must be a scientific explanation for the entity, mustn't there? After all, Palmer's experiments involved drugs, electric shocks, a scientific approach to psychic powers."

"'There are more things in heaven and earth...'" began Percival.

The discussion quickly became heated and somewhat confused. Meanwhile, Paul pondered just how much he should say. He had told no one about his encounter with Liz, or the implicit warning she had delivered.

"You're very quiet about this, Paul," Mia said suddenly, and he saw the lens of Joe Durham's camera swing around to focus on him.

"I—I guess I don't have much to offer," he said, almost truthfully.

"I don't see how anything could destroy Palmer, or what he's become. They should shut off the place completely, forever. Maybe lay a few landmines."

After several hours, Mia thanked them for their help and concluded they had 'some wonderful stuff in the can'. She got each one of the three, including Mike, to verbally commit to another show about Rookwood, with promises of generous fees. As they drove back to the city, Mike and 'Percy' chatted about the TV team. Sitting in back, Paul peered out moodily at the August landscape. England was at its most beautiful in the run-up to harvest time, but he could not enjoy the vista of ripening crops, newly sheared sheep, and fat, contented cattle.

He felt immensely lonely, a man shut off from the rest of the human race. Paul had been lying to Mia, holding back what he knew. He had no intention of involving himself with any more TV shows. He had another purpose in mind altogether. It was not pleasant to deceive people he liked and respected, but it was necessary.

He was prepared to lie to everyone from now on. If he was to achieve what was needed, he could not trust anyone, not even a friend like Mike.

***

Three days after his trip to Northumberland, Paul got an urgent call from Neve Cotter, asking him to come around at once. It was mid-morning, and he expected to find Ella at home. He was surprised when Neve told him her daughter was at school.

"So, Liz isn't back?" he asked, puzzled, as she let him in.

"Ella sometimes sleepwalks," Neve said, leading him through the living room. "She walked into my room last night. I decided not to wake her. This morning she didn't seem to remember anything, so I just took her to school as usual."

Neve led him into her bedroom. Paul felt embarrassed and confused. He saw a large, smiling toy dog among tangled sheets and clothes cast about on the floor. He recalled the neatness of the Cotter's Rookwood apartment, and concluded Neve was too disturbed to tidy up.

"Here," said the woman. "See what she did."

Paul turned around, looked at the dressing table. Ella had written huge, straggling letters on the mirror in her mother's lipstick.

SET ME FREE—DESTROY IT!

"You understand this, don't you?" Neve demanded. Her voice was low, tense, accusatory.

"Yes," he said quietly. "She's been quite patient with me. But now I have to do something."

Neve looked at him for a few moments, and he felt ashamed. His cowardice, his desperate hope some other solution might miraculously appear, had endangered a child. Ella's life might not be at risk, but her future was.

"It's a shot across the bows, I guess," Paul said heavily. "A warning that I have to do something. Something decisive."

He felt the room start to spin, and Neve gripped him tightly by the arm, led him to the living room couch. He kept apologizing until she told him to shut up and made him some tea. She offered to put a shot of vodka in it, but he turned it down. Paul sat staring at the TV set. The sound was turned down, and a news program was showing rioting somewhere. People screamed, tear gas or smoke billowed, placards waved. Then they cut to the football coverage.

"One life isn't so much, is it?" he said, half to himself, as Neve handed him a steaming mug. "Why make such a fuss about it?"

"Hey," Neve said sharply. "I've had my doubts about religion, but I still think life is sacred—even the most despised of us count for something. Where there's life, there's hope."

She reached out and laid a hand on his arm. For the first time, he felt no disapproval from her. Instead, he saw sympathy and understanding in her slightly wan features.

"It's not fair," she said quietly. "For any of us. I don't know why you or I or Ella got tangled up in this. But we did. Let me try and help. I'd do anything to protect her, you know that."

Paul felt a sudden, surprising joy at the fact that this woman, who hardly knew him, and had no reason to put her faith in him, would make such an offer. The mire of depression that had dragged him low over the past weeks became less oppressive. In that moment, he felt truly alive, and in charge of his destiny, not a slave to it.

"No," he said. "She needs you more than anything in the world, right now. And I've made my choice. I guess I made it a while back. I just needed reminding."

CHAPTER 9

Liz left him and Ella alone once his purpose was clear. Six days later he was ready.

He left it until late at night, just after one in the morning. As he stole out to the car, he thought of Mike on sabbatical, enjoying his time in the archives of King's College, Cambridge. It was a happy coincidence there was no one to notice as Paul snuck out on his mission. Paul remembered the beautiful city as he had first seen it; caught in morning sunlight, a living monument to civilization, learning, sanity. He hoped Mike would understand, and that his friend would be able to forgive him.

The old Peugeot started the first time for once, and Paul steered it carefully out of the street onto the almost empty highway. Doing this at night meant his inexperience with right-hand drive vehicles would not be so hazardous. He also felt it was somehow appropriate to approach Rookwood in darkness. But first, he needed more basic ingredients.

He drove to the outskirts of Tynecastle and pulled into a small gas station. Paul filled up the Peugeot's tank, then bought two extra cans of gasoline. He put the cans in the trunk, next to the special package in a hold all. He had already purchased some other ingredients, paying cash at a number of different stores, having spent a little while surfing the web incognito for data. He had no idea if British security agencies like MI5 or GCHQ would routinely flag up such activity. It seemed unlikely. The internet was awash with dangerous knowledge, easily acquired. And anyway, he doubted Farson's superiors would have put a deranged American history professor on a terror watch list.

If I'm wrong, they could be following me right now.

Paul looked around, but saw nobody in or around the gas station, except for a guy chatting with the girl at the checkout. Both seemed bored, weary. He wondered if each was longing for their shift to end. He wondered how they would feel if they knew what he was preparing to do. And how much danger they were in right now. Then the girl turned around, started doing something on the shelves behind her counter. It seemed rude, to ignore the man right in front of her. Then the man stopped talking, and faded away.

A lonely ghost, he thought. *Will I ever stop seeing them? Or will I just get used to it?*

Paul shrugged off the thought, focused on the task at hand, but resisted the temptation to open the trunk again to check its contents. If he did that, he might start fiddling with the device he had made. It was a very crude bomb, but it was the best a not-very-practical man with a humanities background could manage at relatively short notice. Slowly gathering components—timers, detonators, and so forth—would risk exposure at any moment. Far better, he had reasoned, to get everything done as quickly as possible.

He was going to destroy Rookwood, or as much of it as he could. The plan was to blow up the East Wing with a combined explosive and incendiary bomb. Paul knew there was a small, but very real, chance he would blow himself to pieces before he could get clear. But as the time had grown nearer, he had found himself less concerned with his own survival. He wondered if everyone setting out to do something highly illegal and destructive felt as he did—the sense of clarity, the indifference to everyday concerns.

Is this how a terrorist feels when they're about to commit an atrocity?

He got back into Mike's car, trying to shove aside the thought. He was not, after all, going to kill anyone. The target was empty, legally. He knew it was full of the unquiet dead. It would always be a place of danger to anyone who entered it. He wanted to send the essence of Doctor Miles Rugeley Palmer to Hell if he could, but felt the best he could hope for would be to simply disperse the Palmer entity.

He drove out of the gas station and tried to concentrate on the road ahead. A small van appeared from a side street and darted across the main road. Paul swerved, pumping the brakes. His over-reaction might have caused a major pile-up in daylight on these ever-busy English roads. He sat, breath rasping, for a few seconds before taking his foot off the brake. He had been right to drive in the small hours.

Resuming his journey, he was soon in the leafy suburbs on Blaydon Avenue. By night, the area looked pleasant, serene even. But as soon as he saw Rookwood, his gut tightened and his mouth grew dry. He glanced at his rear-view mirror, checking nobody was close behind. He was gambling on few witnesses and a slow response from the famously under-resourced local cops.

The gates were shut, of course. He had checked out the location a few times, and nothing seemed to be going on. There was certainly no living person on the premises, just the security guard in his lonely little booth by the gates. Paul drove straight between the gateposts, glimpsing the open-mouthed guard raising his walkie-talkie. He prayed the Peugeot would not stall or simply fall apart as it smashed into the wrought-iron gates. They looked relatively flimsy, more ornamental than protective.

The impact flung him forward, winding him, and pain shot through his ribs as the seatbelt cut into his body. But the gates gave way, one swinging back while the other was wrenched from its hinges and fell to the ground. Paul careered up the driveway, praying the old car would not stall on him, swerved past the main entrance, and headed for the East Wing. He stopped, sized up the target, which was a regular sized doorway. This must be a weak point, he reasoned, as a door is basically a hole. And if he hit it hard enough, the car would end up inside.

Which is a problem, he thought. Because being inside would leave him exposed to the entity's full power. Fear was already churning his stomach. He could almost feel the unearthly cold; Palmer's grip closing on his mind. If he fell under the entity's control he would die, one way or another. Perhaps he might even thwart his own plan.

"Liz?" he said aloud as he reversed quickly onto the turf. "Liz, are you with me? Will you cover me while I do this?"

He paused for a moment as the car came to a halt, hoping for a fall in temperature. There was no sign of any paranormal presence, however, so Paul got out after popping the trunk, and ran around to set the crude timer. He heard a distant siren howling and cursed as he fumbled with the digital clock. The near-empty roads would help the cops get to him all the faster, he realized. It was one of many things he had not thought about, so focused had Paul been on ending the entity. He gave it five minutes, then changed his mind and went for four.

Paul climbed back in, buckled up, and gunned the engine with the handbrake on, feeling absurd, a passive man playing an action-hero role. He still saw no sign of anything unusual, felt no sudden chill. He released the parking brake and the car slewed forward across the turf, over the gravel pathway, and smashed into the doorway. There was a jolt, much more severe than when he had rammed the gates. Then the car was inside the East Wing.

The engine died, as did the headlights. Paul sat motionless in the darkness, hearing the hiss of escaping steam or air, feeling a dull thud as something fell onto the roof above him. The windshield, he saw as his eyes adjusted, was apparently covered in plaster dust. He unfastened his seatbelt and tried to open the door.

It was jammed shut.

Of course it's stuck, he thought, feeling oddly calm. *Despite spending weeks thinking this over, I didn't once think of what might happen if I bashed a car right into a brick wall. Silly me.*

He leaned over, tried the passenger side door. It opened about two inches before it slammed against intact brickwork. He started to feel panic rising but remembered a few things he had seen on TV. He groped for the lever that would let him slide the seat back, found it after what seemed an age, and pushed hard. It was still a tight fit, but he could raise his legs, kick at the windshield.

It must be down to three minutes, now.

He kicked a second time, a third, both feet close together. The windshield, probably weakened by the impact, flew out in one piece. Paul bruised himself badly as he scrambled to get out. He slid over the hood of the Peugeot and landed on hands and knees in what felt like a heap of rubble. Something cut his hand, and he cursed, but kept moving. The wall had collapsed right up to roof level, so he could clamber out over the top of the car. And once he was outside the actual walls of Rookwood, he would be safe.

But, once he managed to scramble onto the roof of the Peugeot, he saw the way back to safety was blocked.

The distant streetlights of Blaydon Avenue were the only source of illumination and were feeble at best. But Paul could still see something moving between him and the row of distant, diffuse lamps. He could make out a tall figure, far taller than a man. And with it came a sudden, intense panic that banished all calm and undermined his self-control. He froze, heard himself whimper in fear. He felt, as much as heard, heavy footsteps coming closer.

Now he could make out horns or antlers atop the dark figure's huge head.

Cernunnos, Pan, the god of the forest.

Paul struggled to keep himself from screaming, fought against the instinct to flee, which would have sent him back into the East Wing. A tiny, rational corner of his mind told him he was right on the boundary between Palmer's domain and the relative safety of the outer world.

But the nature god was waiting for him.

"I—I'm doing this for you," he stammered. "You h-hate him as much as I do."

The dark form was motionless now, and Paul felt sure it was looking at him, if such a being could be said to see in any regular way. He sensed a slight easing of the aura of fright, felt himself able to move again. He pulled himself forward along the Peugeot's buckled roof. The strange deity remained motionless, but now Paul saw its outline flicker and blur a little.

Behind him, the rubble stirred. A sudden, piercing cold gripped his feet, calves, worked its way up his legs. The Palmer entity, rather belatedly, was reaching out. Trying to suppress resurgent panic, Paul hurled himself onto the trunk of the Peugeot. As he slid off onto the gravel of the driveway, he imagined his crude bomb, inches away from his face, the digital clock ticking down.

He had no idea how much time had elapsed since he had set the detonator. Behind him, he heard more debris stirring. He looked up and saw a huge face sweeping down toward him and felt profoundly grateful he could see no expression in the gloom.

"No!" he shouted, holding up a hand that was tiny beside the vast, dark visage.

The looming figure faded away, and with it the terror it had brought. His fear lessened into a desire for self-preservation. He ran without looking back, deciding to head for the gates and let the security guard grab him if the guy felt like it.

The Peugeot exploded, a geyser of flame engulfing much of the East Wing. Old plastic sheets left by builders were flung into the air, caught fire, and fell onto the grass. Paul, caught in a searing shockwave, staggered forward, then turned to look at his handiwork, covering his face with one arm. He felt his eyebrows get singed. A globe of orange and red flame was rising above the East Wing, disappearing as he watched. Debris showered down around him, something struck him on the head and he felt pain, then the warmth of blood. He fell a few paces back and saw a great sheet of flame belching smoke from the ten-foot gap in the wall.

I did it, he thought. *I actually did it. I hit back at the bastard, big time.*

Paul's emotional numbness returned as he waited. Within a couple of minutes, the fire had caught hold, and much of the East Wing was ablaze. Paul stood back, surveying his handiwork with satisfaction as he dabbed his wounded head with a tissue. Flames were spreading to the main block of the building, woodwork catching alight, the now intense heat doing its work. He felt a sense of grim satisfaction. He might have been a sloppy bomber and an inept arsonist, but he had at least got the job done.

The howling of a siren made him turn to face Blaydon Avenue. Sure enough, two police cars turned in at the gates, tore up the driveway, then halted about twenty yards away. Paul guessed the officers were unsure of how dangerous he was and weren't willing to simply come forward and confront what might be an armed maniac. He knew British police sometimes carried firearms in their vehicles and wondered for a moment if they would shoot him down without ceremony. It seemed doubtful. If there was one thing he had learned about this country, it was that a blast of gunfire was seldom seen as an ideal solution to anything.

Paul turned back to survey his handiwork, hoping the blaze would destroy it all, but was resigned to some of Rookwood surviving. He hoped Palmer would be terminally weakened, if not destroyed, whatever the outcome. A slightly different siren, deeper and less frantic sounding, was growing louder now, and he recognized it as a fire engine. Presumably, he would be arrested any minute.

"Armed police! Put your hands above your head!"

Paul felt some relief at the command bellowed through a megaphone. He did as he was told, still facing the fire, feeling emotionally numb. The heat was growing intense, and he felt sure the blaze would be difficult to extinguish. There was no sense of triumph or fulfillment, only a vague hope he might have made a difference. If the fire had done enough damage, then the old asylum would probably be demolished. And, given the track record of Rookwood apartments, it seemed unlikely anything would be built on the site.

It would make a nice park, he thought. *They could plant more trees, flowers, the usual stuff.*

The thought of Rookwood returned to something like its natural state should have been pleasant, reassuring. But instead, Paul felt a sudden pang of doubt and wondered if he had in fact done the right thing at all. The roof collapsed with a tremendous crash, then Paul started as a hand touched his shoulder.

"Come on sir, show me your hands, please."

A young policewoman was standing beside him, taser in hand. Paul glanced around and saw two male officers pointing pistols at him. They all looked nervous, faces pale in the flickering light of the fire. He lowered his hands slowly, held them out, wrists together.

"I'll come quietly," he told the young woman, who took out a set of handcuffs and clicked them on.

"Good to know," she replied. Then, nodding at the blaze, she asked, "What the hell did you do?"

"Tried to purge the place of—a bad influence," Paul said. "It's a long story."

The fire siren was too close for him to hear the woman's next remark. They all turned to look at the huge, red vehicle slowly negotiating the tight turn into the grounds of Rookwood. The siren, mercifully, went silent, just in time for Paul to hear one of the male officer's exclamation.

"What the hell is that?"

They turned back to look at the East Wing. Something was moving in the flames, something big, misshapen, definitely too big to be human, even if a human could have lived through that inferno. Fragments of brick and plaster were hurled upward before falling back into the blaze. Then a snake-like form reared up, wove back and forth, as if blindly seeking a way out of the inferno. Another sinuous shape appeared, and a third.

Are they ropes? Paul wondered. *No, they must be electrical cables! Maybe Palmer's essence is bound up with them in some way.*

Fragments of masonry and metal started to accumulate around the cables as they began to plait themselves together. Paul stepped back a few more paces, baffled and appalled. The fabric of Rookwood Asylum, he knew, must be permeated with psychic energy. Paul guessed the Palmer entity, desperate to survive, was trying to build a body for itself from the debris of its blazing home. It had failed to break free before using human vessels, but maybe this would be more effective.

"Oh crap," he murmured.

"What's that?" the policewoman asked, eyes wide.

"The evil influence," Paul said quickly, then found himself shouting commands at the police. "Move back, get well away from it! It probably can't escape, but we can't be sure."

The cops did not need any more urging. They backed away, and he tried to follow, but stumbled on the ruts the Peugeot's tires had torn up. With his wrists cuffed, he fell heavily, and found himself on his back, gazing up at the bizarre colossus. Now it had a definite man-like figure, albeit misshapen, standing around thirty feet high. The limbs were of uneven lengths, the head oversized, the body an ill-defined mass of wires and masonry fragments.

The head turned and Paul sensed it peering down at him. He saw the familiar flicker of two glass discs in the pitch-black 'face'. It lifted one of its half-made legs and took a stride toward him. Paul heard shouting, confusion, one of the officers trying to give orders. But in the roar of the flames and the crash of the advancing giant, it was hard to make out words.

The Palmer entity took another step, debris falling away from its body, fresh matter swirling up to replenish the losses. Paul could sense it, feel the power radiating from the concentrated essence of Palmer's immense ego, his intense need to amass power and dominate others.

There was a loud pop, then another. Paul realized one of the cops was shooting at the thing, but there was no hint of any damage. The entity took another step, this time the huge, misshapen foot was clearly outside the now-ruined wall of the building. Paul began to skootch away on his butt, tried to get upright, fell again. The grotesque thing took another step, so Palmer's incarnation of metal and brick and plastic was looming over him. A hand, copper ligaments gleaming in the flames, reached down toward him.

"Liz! Liz, help me!" he screamed.

A jet of water shot over him and struck the monster in its face. Chunks of black matter were stripped away and hurled back into the flames. More nondescript matter rose from the inferno to repair the damage, but it was too little, and Palmer's new body was being worn away. Paul twisted around and saw firefighters aiming the powerful jet, the police standing by, gawping like any civilian. He looked back at the grotesque figure and saw it reeling back, one arm held up to try and ward off the water. The Palmer entity continued to lose its hastily concocted tissue and sinew as it retreated into the flames, and then collapsed with a shower of sparks.

"I wouldn't let him hurt you," said a familiar voice.

He felt something touch his shoulder and looked up to see a gray-clad girl kneeling behind him. She smiled down at Paul, moved her hand from his shoulder to his face. The coolness of her touch was not piercing, it brought no discomfort. Instead, it proved a relief from the heat beating against his face and body.

"I dropped a hint to those brave lads," she went on, nodding at the firefighters, who were now spraying water liberally over the East Wing. "Not difficult. They'd probably have thought of it themselves a second or two later."

"Maybe a second too late," Paul said. "Liz, did it work? What happened to Palmer?"

But Liz was already gone. In her place, the young woman officer was looking down at him in wide-eyed puzzlement, holding out her hand. As she helped him up, she asked Paul what had just happened. There was a hint of pleading in her voice.

"Officially," he replied, with a grin, "I doubt anything happened at all. Or are you going to sign a report with a giant monster in it?"

He was led to the nearest patrol car and put in the back seat. On the ride back into Tynecastle he heard the young woman talking to another officer on the radio. It took them about thirty seconds to decide someone had fired 'a couple of warning shots into the air'.

"After all," she said, "it was all over in a couple of seconds. We can't be sure what we saw. And nor can the fire service guys."

Paul did not care. He had wrecked the heart of Palmer's power, his principal domain, the place where he had worked, tormented his victims, and died. The East Wing would have to be torn down, and quite possibly the rest of Rookwood. He leaned back, felt tension ebb away. It was an odd sensation for someone who had just been arrested and would probably face an arson charge.

The patrol car turned off Blaydon Avenue and passed a municipal park. The headlights picked out masses of leaves, a small pavilion, ornamental gates. Again, Paul thought of what might happen if Rookwood were wholly demolished. He wished he could talk to someone about it.

"Is there any way I could call someone?" he asked. "A friend, maybe—I don't have a lawyer."

"That's okay, mate," said the officer sitting beside him. "If you need a lawyer, you'll get one. Since you're behaving yourself—and thanks for that, by the way—it shouldn't take long to get you processed. Then we'll call the duty psychiatrist, and he'll examine you. Nothing personal, it is routine in a case like this..."

The young cop paused, looked at Paul more closely.

"Here," he said, "aren't you that American bloke who was there when that actor died?"

The rest of the journey was dominated by a discussion of Inspector Grist from the viewpoint of real-life police work.

***

"I wish I could remember," Paul said. "You'd think something like that would be etched in your memory, but I just can't recall it, not precisely. "

"Remember what, Paul?" asked the therapist.

Paul, who had been talking to himself, looked up, momentarily surprised to see the man sitting opposite.

"Sorry," he said. "Rambling again. Maybe it's these pills you put me on. They kind of blur the edges of everything."

The therapist gave a little smile. The office was small, less classy than that of Doctor Blume, but that was because Paul was now going through the criminal justice system. He had been diagnosed as unfit to plead in a regular trial and had been committed for a few weeks under mental health laws. Then he was released to return home and continue living with Mike.

That brought its own problems. Tynecastle University had finally dispensed with Paul's services. People prone to blowing up large buildings were seen as a liability, it seemed. The meager savings Paul had was rapidly dwindling, and he was already fending off Mike's generosity on a regular basis. The only real option for Paul was to accept Mia Callan's offer of another fee. She was, predictably, delighted at the latest twist in the Rookwood saga, and wanted 'the inside story' on what Paul had done, and why. She had assured him he could well become the media's 'go-to guy' on all things paranormal. The idea did not fill him with joy.

He was happy to share all of these concerns with his court-appointed therapist. It helped him avoid going too deeply into the darker, stranger truths that had brought him to the kind therapist's office. He had seen something, he knew, amid the confusion when the blaze took hold, the police appeared, and the firefighters got to work. It was a detail, and it might well have been utterly irrelevant.

Or it might not, he thought, as his subconscious failed to dredge up the memory for the hundredth time.

***

"Still can't remember the details of that night?" asked Mike. "Well, maybe it doesn't matter. They're demolishing it, the whole building—you do know that?"

"Yes," Paul said, feeling only slight impatience. "My memory's okay, I just feel—warm and fuzzy. Happy pills have turned me into a robot, or something like it. I feel as if I'm running myself on some kind of remote control."

Mike gave Paul a tentative pat on the arm.

"They gave you a course of, what, three months? Soon be over. Also, got a surprise for you."

Mike took a key fob from his pocket, and a few yards away, a neat silver car unlocked its doors and flashed its sidelights.

"No more taxis," the Englishman explained. "Got a good deal on a second-hand Corolla."

Paul launched into yet another apology, but as before, Mike waved it aside. Paul had, apparently, done his friend 'a favor' by getting rid of the Peugeot. It was typical of the man, and Paul felt more upset by this kindness than any possible reproach. The nagging doubt at the back of his mind continued to worry away at him as well.

They got in and Mike set off, steering his new car into the midday traffic. As his friend extolled the virtues of the Corolla, Paul made polite noises, but continued obsessing over the blurred memories of the fateful night. He closed his eyes, and the body the Palmer entity had constructed for itself rose up before him again as Mike cursed a cab driver.

But what about the head?

The hand with its copper wire claws was clear in his mind's eye—he could see it reaching for him, out of the flames of the asylum. He could also remember the overall shape of the Palmer entity's hastily contrived body. He saw its asymmetric limbs flailing as the fire hose knocked it back. But the head—the head was just a black polygon, ill-defined, so he could not be sure.

Had antlers, of a sort, sprouted from that head, just before the Palmer entity had collapsed into the blazing ruins? Or had Paul simply confabulated that half-memory after the event, his confusion increased by post-traumatic stress, not to mention the powerful medication he was on?

"Goddamn it, I can't be sure," said Paul, under his breath. "I just can't be sure."

"What?" asked Mike, breaking off his cheery monologue. "You all right, bud?"

"Yeah," said Paul. "Just tired, I guess."

CHAPTER 10

"She's gone, then?" Paul said quietly.

Neve Cotter shrugged.

"If she's not gone for good, she's on an extended vacation."

Paul and Neve were walking along the promenade overlooking the beach at the seaside resort of Tynemouth. The sands were crowded with sunbathers, the screams of children vying with those of seagulls fighting over discarded fish and chips. Ahead of them, Ella Cotter carefully held an ice cream to prevent white driblets going down her arm. Mike was pointing to a distant lighthouse, telling a story of shipwreck and heroism. Ella was enduring it politely.

"No marks on her arms, I noticed," Paul said. "And she seems happy enough."

A gull swooped down toward Ella's ice cream, and Mike tried to fend it off, waving his jacket at the shrieking bird. Ella took a step back and wolfed down her treat in a couple of seconds. The gull backed off, and Mike proudly took credit for 'repelling the airborne threat'.

"It's good to have normal crises," Neve said. "I'm worried about her getting sunburned, for instance. And how she'll do on her SATS test this autumn. Normal mother stuff."

They walked on in awkward silence for a while. Paul was acutely aware other people might think they were a couple who were having a holiday falling out. His mind was less muzzy now, thanks to a reduction in his medication. Work had begun on the demolition of the remains of Rookwood, which was pronounced too smoke and fire damaged to be saved. So far, nothing unusual had occurred. Paul wondered if he could genuinely put the whole bizarre affair behind him.

"I got a call from Mia Callan, again," Neve said. "She wanted to talk about Liz, Ella, you. Of course, I said no. She promised discretion, no real names used, that kind of thing. But there's already enough online chatter about—about it all. I want to fade into the background with Ella, live a normal life."

"She's very persistent," Paul said, sympathetically. "Like a seagull with an ice cream, she just zeroes in—single-minded. I guess that's a virtue in her world."

"It also seems to be a virtue in Liz's world," Neve responded. "Though perhaps she's in another world now."

Paul mulled that over. It was a thought that had often occurred to him. It seemed apt that Liz, the only one of Palmer's victims to resist him after death, should have reached some kind of heaven or nirvana. But he had learned to doubt such instincts. He had, after all, assumed Liz was finally free of Rookwood when she met her long-lost daughter, Sharon. But that had been a false dawn.

On the other hand, there was the matter of the ghosts. Since his attack on the old asylum, he had not been seeing the dead. Or at least, he assumed so. He had certainly not seen Mrs. Ratbag's husband, or any other figures who were quite clearly apparitions. He glanced up and down the promenade, wondering if any of the people enjoying the August weather were ghosts. It seemed unlikely. The disappearance of the unwanted 'talent' could be a sign things had returned to normal.

Whatever that is, he thought.

"We want to build a sandcastle," said Mike, bringing Paul back to the present.

"Mike wants to build a sandcastle," Ella corrected. "I said I am willing to help."

"In a supervisory capacity, of course," added Mike. "Or we could go and look in some rock pools, maybe find some crabs, that sort of thing?"

Paul smiled at his friend's enthusiasm. Soon, they were down on the beach, Mike, having purchased a cheap bucket and spade, and seeking damp sand 'of the right consistency' under Ella's supervision. It was a perfect summer's day, and as they messed around, Paul sometimes forgot Palmer and Rookwood. Occasionally, he forgot it all for minutes at a time.

***

Lance Percival's cleaner had just left. With a sigh, he set down his mug of strong Assam tea and looked around the living room. He had done his best to avoid leaving any obvious targets for tidying up. But he could already see that a couple of Folklore Society pamphlets were shoved, upside down, onto the wrong shelf.

"Perhaps if I pay her some kind of bonus," he mused. "A pound for everything she *doesn't* tidy up. No, that wouldn't work, arrant lunacy. Or I could pay her to make things less tidy, throw a few books onto the sofa? No, no, that would merely encourage total anarchy. It seems there is no solution..."

Percival began to putter around, rescuing the pamphlets and placing them on a pile of related leaflets next to the television. Then he started to examine some stacks of books that had been disarranged while being vigorously dusted. As always happened, Percival stumbled across a volume he hadn't read in years, sometimes one he had totally forgotten about. On this particular autumn morning, the book was remarkably pertinent to his earlier researches.

"Good Lord," he murmured, thinking back to his last meeting with Michael Bryson and his American friend. Paul Mahan had seemed distracted, a little out of it, but that was to be expected. The important thing was everyone was all right. Feeling some small pride in his role in the affair, he checked the book's table of contents.

"Just what I need! Or at least, just what I would have needed a few weeks ago. Such is life, I suppose. Quite fascinating, regardless."

He forgot about his de-tidying efforts and sat down again, took another mouthful of tea, and began to leaf through *Gods & Demons of Old England,* by Darrell Pardoe, Ph.D. Soon he was lost in accounts of strange beliefs, bizarre rituals, and lethal forces unleashed by the unwary. He had quite forgotten why he had wanted the book in the first place and was simply enjoying its wonders for their own sake. It was a wonderful sensation.

He heard a rustling sound, looked up, saw nothing that might have rustled. Percival shrugged, went back to the book. Then there was a creaking noise, and something fell heavily. He knew it was probably a book, given that ninety percent of his possessions were books.

"Mice?" he said to himself. "Rats?"

It seemed unlikely. He wondered if a neighbor's cat had snuck in, perhaps following the cleaner? But a cat, he felt, would be more likely to make its presence felt by meowing, begging for food, or perhaps scratching great chunks out of his library. The thought of an animal destroying his precious possessions galvanized the old man, and he jumped up out of his chair, listening intently for the next movement.

"Lance."

The voice hissed in his right ear, but when he spun around clumsily, there was no one there. Yet he had a distinct feeling he was not alone, a sensation of cold fingers running up his spine. It was not the first time he had felt something spooky, but it had never happened in his cozy little apartment before.

"Lance, this is the end."

The voice came from his left side, now, as if some unseen person were dancing around him, mocking him. The cold was more intense now, and he shuddered, almost hugged himself against the chill.

"Nonsense!" he snapped. "Over-active imagination."

With a startling clatter, a whole shelf load of books fell to the floor. Percival was still searching for the creature, any creature, that might have been loose in the room. But as the piercing cold grew, he had to abandon the idea. It was obvious what was present. Something that should not have been able to leave its lair at Rookwood. Something that Percival had assumed was gone for good.

"Yes, Lance," came the voice, this time emanating from the bookshelf. *"You took so much interest in me, I've come to see you. And*

all your wonderful books."

Percival gasped in horror as the fallen books floated upward, drifting ever faster through the air in arcs, swirling around as if caught in a silent tornado. As the old man looked on, frozen in shock, the disparate volumes started to disintegrate, pages ripped free of bindings, dustjackets torn off, a confetti of yellowed paper bursting out from the mutilated tomes. Lint and dust flowed up and into the swirling mass.

"No!" he cried.

"Oh yes," mocked the voice from the paper vortex. *"First your precious books, then your feeble, bookish soul."*

Gods & Demons of Old England leaped from his chair to join the dusty maelstrom. Other objects hurled themselves across the room into the spinning column of paper and cardboard. A human-like form began to evolve from the chaos of torn print, limbs and a head growing from the original cloud. Framed photographs, a phone handset, an old pair of slippers, a forgotten mug. A random assortment of pens and pencils formed crude, claw-like fingers. Wires torn from the TV and radio combined with pulped paper to create stunted horns or antlers.

I was right, Percival thought, intellectual curiosity still active despite his terror. *Palmer did merge with the ancient god. And between them, they've broken free of their old bonds. But surely, they can't last long with no power base, no source of energy?*

The entity did not look as if it was running low on power, however. Percival ran, or tried to, stumbling toward the door as his heart pounded wildly under his ribcage. He could not tear his gaze away from the entity, which was now almost solid, no longer spinning, but coalescing rapidly into a body. It was so large it's misshapen head swept against the ceiling. It took a single, huge stride across the small room, and Percival yelped in terror, ducked through the open door into the short hallway. He felt its talons rake down his back, almost fell, then made it to the front door. He not only had to save himself, he had to tell others.

"Old man, you can't get away."

It was true. A vast limb, light brown and speckled with print, encircled Percival's chest, and lifted him easily off the floor. The Palmer entity turned him around in mid-air, and then he was face to face with it, saw the gleam of the long-dead doctor's spectacles that had been described to him so many times. The thing raised its other arm, the four-fingered hand glittering with pointed metal.

The frenzied beating of Percival's heart was transformed into a blossoming agony that took hold of his entire left side. He saw the nightmare visage twist into a smile, fragments of paper falling away from the huge, lopsided mouth. A roaring in his ears grew, and his vision darkened. He felt himself being allowed to slide to the hall carpet, the remains of dozens of precious books falling around him, a blizzard of ruined knowledge.

"Now we are one!"

The pain ebbed, vanished. The vicious cold remained. Percival looked down at the body of a small, skinny man in a faded dressing gown and covered in torn paper. He recognized himself. Around him, faces gathered, all contorted with rage and madness. They gradually coalesced into one face, someone he had seen before in old films and photographs. Palmer's smug, plump visage grew until it filled the dark, cold universe. Percival, trying to scream, felt the merciless power pulling him toward the entity. Still trying to scream, he fell into it.

***

The memorial service saw a 'good turnout for the old chap', as Mike put it. There were well-chosen readings by friends from academe, Mike included, and by Percival's daughter and grown-up grandchildren. Paul was somewhat surprised to have been invited, but Mike explained he had been asked to advise on the matter.

"I was his star student, a long time ago," he said, with a sad smile. "Apparently, he mentioned me in his will, said I should be consulted, that kind of thing."

Paul nodded, scanning the crowd of dark-clad, mostly older people. One person who stood out like a sore thumb was Detective Sergeant Farson, who was just leaving the small chapel. Paul excused himself and set off in pursuit, catching up with the officer in the car park of the crematorium. Farson was lighting up a cigarette.

"You'd be surprised how many of us smoke," he remarked, seeing Paul's expression. "Relieves stress, provides a psychological crutch, all that jazz.

"I'm surprised to see you here," Paul said. "You weren't involved with the investigation, were you?"

Farson looked over Paul's shoulder. Some mourners had followed them outside and were within earshot. The detective led Paul over to a shadowed corner of the parking lot, out of sight of the crematorium doorway.

"Officially, no," he conceded. "But we have our unofficial ways to stay informed. As soon as I knew there was a link to you, I took an interest."

Paul waited, knowing Farson would say exactly as much as he wanted and no more.

"So, the first uniforms on the scene thought it was a break-in that went wrong," Farson went on. "There was a mess, stuff thrown around, books torn up. And the old guy was dead in his hallway, massive coronary. The idea was one or more local junkies had broken in and turned the place over looking for cash. When they didn't find any, they tried to force the old man to hand over his money, or other valuables, by torturing his books. It has a kind of twisted logic to it. Fits the facts, up to a point. However, there was also a series of parallel wounds on his back, something had been used to cut through his clothing."

Farson took another drag on his half-smoked cigarette, then threw it down and stamped on it.

"Filthy habit, gonna try and give it up again," he remarked. "Anyway, the front door lock was damaged, wood splintered, the actual door standing slightly ajar. That was what alerted one of the neighbors when she came home from work. But—and this bothers me, I must admit—there were no fingerprints, not even a partial, anywhere in the apartment. It's odd. Thugs in search of money for their next hit don't usually run to subtleties like gloves. That's more an organized crime thing. And retired professors don't tend to fall foul of gangsters, right?"

Paul nodded. He had heard some these facts via Mike, who had, in turn, got them from Percival's relatives. From the start, he had doubted whether the old man's death had been the result of regular crime. But he had, perversely, hoped it could be so. Far better to believe Percival was the victim of mere humans, however depraved, than accept that the Palmer entity could have sought him out. Because that would mean the vile thing had somehow broken free of its captivity in Rookwood.

"But what do you think?" Paul asked. "Honestly, is there any link to what—to what's happened at Rookwood?"

Farson shrugged, looked past Paul. There was a growing hubbub of conversation as people filed out of the chapel, the sound of car doors slamming, engines starting. When Farson spoke again, his question was surprising.

"You probably deal with library catalogs quite a lot? Or did, in your lecturing days?"

Paul nodded, wondering where this was going.

"It's a little out of my wheelhouse," Farson continued. "But I had a look at Percival's list of his own books, during a discreet visit to the scene. Then I checked the ones that were missing in action—the ones that had been shredded. Interesting correlation, I felt. And I think this is my ride, so I'll bid you farewell. For now."

A dark blue, unmarked sedan had drawn up just outside the parking lot. Farson walked briskly over to it and got in the front. As the vehicle disappeared Paul went back to the chapel to rejoin Mike and share what he had just been told.

***

"Funeral for a friend?" asked the driver.

"Nah," Farson replied. "Loose ends, an ongoing case."

"Right, right. The Rookwood thing."

Farson glanced over at the driver, and thought he detected the hint of a smile on the man's face.

"Something amusing you, Eric?" he asked. "Care to share?"

Eric, newly promoted to Detective Constable, knew better than to be evasive with a superior who had cut him a good bit of slack in the past.

"It's just that, some of the guys—they think you've gone a bit, I dunno, off the reservation on this one."

Farson felt anger rising, but also confusion. He had done his best after being allocated the Jeff Bowman case. Instead of being a nice, neat death with a moral overtone—domestic abuser dies during attempt to abduct child—it had turned into a mare's nest of weird, unmanageable claims and counterclaims.

"They still calling me Spooky Farson in the canteen, then, Eric?" he asked, keeping his voice quiet and level.

"It's just a few idiots," Eric shot back, a little too quickly. "You know how it is, mate, nobody means anything by it."

"Keep your eyes on the road, Eric."

Farson seethed silently for a half mile or so. He thought of all the weird stuff that inevitably landed on his desk, now that he was 'the Rookwood guy'. He had tried to hand off the bundle of linked cases to junior officers but had been refused. Then he had begun arguing there was nothing criminal to investigate. But his boss, who did not like ambitious, clever underlings, had decided there was enough evidence of 'suspicious activity' to keep the various files open. Farson was given other cases, of course, but these invariably were weak tea, minor stuff anyone could have handled.

It was a classic Catch-22, or so Farson thought. Various people had been killed and injured; a bomb had gone off. But the only explanation connecting it all was inadmissible in a court of law. If he subscribed to the paranormal explanation, he definitely would be taken off the case. But he would probably never be assigned another one. Every time he thought Rookwood had fallen dormant, that he could focus on normal cases he had a chance of solving, another bizarre incident occurred.

"Sod them, I'll figure it out," he muttered to himself. "I'll show them."

Farson had a sudden sense of liberation. Simply saying the words had, like a magic spell, dispelled the clenched frustration in his gut. As soon as they got back to headquarters, he would begin to put together a solid, detailed file on Rookwood, connecting all the dots between events and individuals. Farson would present his crappy boss with the facts and challenge him to do something, anything, with the findings. Put the ball firmly in the guy's court. He heard an inner monologue urging him on. It felt good.

And if it's a career-ending mistake, so what? It's a shitty career anyway, you know that. Nobody respects the police anymore, not the media, not the public, not even the government. All those cutbacks mean you'll always be overworked and underpaid, and you'll probably die at your desk. Wouldn't you rather work in private security than go on like this indefinitely?

"What?" Eric asked, looking over in concern. "Seriously, don't let them get to you. Everybody knows you're one of the best—"

Farson barely heard his subordinate. Instead, he was picturing himself sitting at a desk in his own office, not some chaotic shared space. He would be running his own agency. He could be his own boss, he felt sure, earning far more money than his police salary. For every person who sneered at him as Spooky Farson, there would be a dozen who wouldn't give a damn, or they may even admire him for standing up to authority.

"I'll do it," he said, grinning at the oncoming traffic. "I'll show them."

"You do that, mate," said Eric, with a touch of uncertainty. "Respect."

As they drove on in silence Farson wondered, for a moment, what could have prompted this about-face? Why had his attitude changed from one of grim, dogged professionalism?

You just reached your breaking point, said a warm, reassuring voice in his head. *You need to put yourself first. Screw your idiot boss.*

"Yeah," he murmured. "Yeah, that must be it."

Then he shivered slightly and turned to Eric again.

"Hey," he said, "I know it's summer and all, but could you turn the aircon down a touch? It's like a meat freezer in here."

***

Sharon McKee was dreaming, restless images cascading through her sleeping brain. She was trapped in a padded cell, manacled to the wall, and she could hear someone coming to get her. Before the door could open, she knew what she would see—a short, plump, white-coated doctor. A figure who might have been reassuring, in different circumstances, with his slightly comical mustache and round, rimless spectacles.

Palmer's coming!

The door opened, and a dark-haired girl walked in. She was dressed in the same stained, ill-fitting robe as Sharon. The newcomer's face was familiar, but she could not recall the girl's name. Then she remembered, not the name, but who the dark-haired girl was.

"Mother!"

The girl walked over to Sharon, knelt down beside her, ran slender fingers through Sharon's gray hair. The cell disappeared, and they were in a forest glade, shafts of sunlight beaming down through lush summer foliage. The sense of dread vanished, replaced by a warm glow of contentment.

"This is the last time I can come and see you," said the girl.

"Liz!" Sharon exclaimed, suddenly remembering. "Liz, why can't you come anymore?"

The dark eyes looked deep into hers. There was sadness on Liz's small, pretty features. She reached out and took her mother's wrinkled cheek in her pale, slender fingers. Sharon felt surprised at how natural it felt, how easy it was to know this teenaged girl was her mother.

"I stayed close to you as long as I could," Liz said. "But I have the chance to escape, to go on somewhere better. I'm finally free of the cells, the walls, the experiments."

"So why do you have to leave me?" Sharon asked, pleadingly. "I never knew you when you were alive!"

"Because if I stay, he might find me again," the pale girl replied. "And he might be strong enough to defeat me next time."

Liz said something else, then stood up, and the sunlight dimmed, took on a wintry quality. A breeze blew through the forest, and leaves began to fall, browning as they fluttered around them. Sharon tried to get up, reaching desperately for her mother, but she could not move. Liz turned and walked away at a sad, sedate pace, and seemed to vanish from view in an instant.

"Don't go!" Sharon said to her empty bedroom.

Dawn was a gray rectangle behind the drapes. Her clock radio told her it was far too early to get up. But she could not simply turn over and go back to sleep, not after such a dream. She sat up slowly, wincing slightly as her arthritic shoulder protested. She climbed out of bed and went into the kitchen.

As she filled her kettle, she grasped the fading details of the dream. The second and last time she had met her mother, and it was already a torn patchwork of images, words, feelings. The forest glade, the wintry light, the parting words. She reached for a notepad she kept on the refrigerator, useful for jotting down shopping lists. By the time the kettle whistled she had scribbled a few phrases.

Only one stood out, troubling and somehow hurtful. The last words Liz had spoken to her had not been about their relationship at all. Sharon thought back to the time she had encountered Liz outside Rookwood, the kindly American who had helped her understand what had drawn her there. Now she was back home, an hour's drive away from that place, and never wanted to go near it again. But she felt obligated to do something with Liz's message. She poured herself a cup of chamomile tea, then started to check her aging cell phone. As she had suspected, she did not have Paul Mahan's number. But she could surely obtain it somewhere.

She sipped her tea, seated at the table, and watched the morning arrive.

"Tell Paul I'm sorry," she said to herself.

Sorry for what?

CHAPTER 11

"This is it," Mike said, putting a small notebook onto Percival's dining room table. "No problem with the family. In fact, they want me to sell his books on their behalf, and I can take my pick of any I want."

Paul picked up the notebook. It was neatly labeled Library Catalog, and when he opened it, he saw familiar lists of titles, authors, publication dates, and other relevant details. Handwritten catalogs were quite rare these days, but in his research, he had seen many historical examples.

"And all the destroyed books were from that one shelf, pretty much?" Paul asked, gesturing at a bookcase.

"Most of them, but not all," Mike said, "which is very selective of the home invaders, whom nobody saw, don't you think?"

"Very," said Paul, sourly.

It took them a while, but it eventually became clear all the books that had been destroyed were linked to local folklore or pagan nature deities. A great fund of knowledge had been ruined, swept up as waste by a clean-up team after the initial investigation.

"And our greatest asset of all, Percy's brain, is now just ashes," Mike said gloomily. "It's so obvious this was Palmer. I mean, it can't be anything else, can it?"

Paul wanted desperately to deny it, to find some way to reject the obvious conclusion. Because it meant he had not only been wrong, he had been disastrously mistaken. Worse, he might have been suckered into doing exactly what the Palmer entity wanted. He tried to explain to Mike.

"What other conclusion could you draw from the facts available, though?" his friend asked. "Liz said destroy it, Rodria said the same. It seems pretty obvious that was the thing to do. You said yourself, the entity was somehow woven into the fabric of the building, especially the electrical system. You destroyed its power base, pretty much. All that survived is now being torn down, junked, or recycled."

Mike paused, then looked more optimistic.

"This murder could be the bastard's last hurrah, a monster lashing out at a weak opponent before it finally dissipates, dies away, whatever. Isn't that possible?"

Paul shrugged.

"I thought—I thought at the last minute the entity might have merged with the old god," Paul blurted out. "I thought I saw the horned god that Percival—that Percy talked about. Just for a moment. I couldn't be sure."

"Oh," breathed Mike. "Oh crap. Well, if that's true, why hasn't Palmer—or whatever we call him now—why hasn't he killed us? Hell, why isn't he cutting a swathe of destruction across the whole city, the whole country, now that he's loose? I may still be right. That monster may be dying, or already dead."

Paul plunged his face into his hands and admitted he didn't know.

"But maybe we shouldn't be too optimistic, Mike. That's not been helpful in the past."

"Okay, so maybe killing us would be too on the nose?" Mike said quietly. "Maybe he's playing a longer game. Testing his powers, biding his time. God, how can we tell what a long-dead maniac is going to do? All bets are off."

Paul looked up.

"Yeah," he said, "we can't know. But we can be sure of one thing— there are still rules to the game. The entity still has its limitations. It may be free of Rookwood, but is it totally free?"

Paul was about to continue, but his phone rang. It was a message from Mia Callan, who had been contacted by Sharon McKee. He felt his heart sink, sure that this would be enlightening, but not in a good way. Five minutes later he got off the phone with Sharon and had an explanation for Mike.

"I got played," he said. "Big time. Liz was less than honest, and I'm assuming Rodria was just doing as he was told, totally dominated by Palmer."

"Figures," Mike said, ashen faced. "He was always a slimy customer. I'm so sorry I involved you with him, mate."

Paul waved the apology away.

"Maybe the best thing we can do for now is try to find some copies of the missing books," he suggested. "And before you say it, yeah, I know—most of them will be long out of print, and few, if any, will be available as ebooks."

Mike sighed.

"That's how things tend to crumble, cookie-wise."

***

Mia Callan and Laura Blaine sat in the gloom of an editing suite, running through the umpteenth edit of *Terror at Rookwood*.

"I still don't love the title," Mia said. "Associations with terrorism, not horror. But we've used horror too often. And maybe it's a bit tacky anyway, given what happened."

Laura suppressed a sigh. Her boss was a picky workaholic, while she thought of herself as a normal human being who liked downtime, drinks, watching dumb movies, chilling with friends. But somehow, they worked well as a team. Now Mia was obsessing over a few details of the feature-length episode, and the title was the main bugbear.

Laura had mulled this over and settled on a clever ploy, or at least she hoped it would prove fairly smart.

"Hey," she said, as she adjusted the contrast on a murky piece of footage from a hand-held camera. "How about playing it subtle?"

Mia frowned.

"How do you mean? Nothing too Victorian, none of that 'Phantoms of the Madhouse' stuff Lucas—"

The director trailed off, and Laura felt a slight pang of guilt. She had never really liked Lucas, who had looked openly at her butt rather too often for her taste. But, like Mia, she kept forgetting the old guy was dead, and that they had run away rather than try to help him. No matter if they had had a damn good reason to escape. It would always feel cowardly, shoddy.

"No," Laura said mildly. "I was thinking of keeping it factual. Rookwood Asylum. How about that? The name is already out there, after all. There's no sign of online interest flagging."

"And that's what counts," Mia added, thoughtfully. "Yeah, we've been thinking old school, worrying about some network executive vetoing our project. But we're producing it, and if they don't want to buy it, tough. We can sell it via any one of a dozen webcasting platforms. Hell, at a pinch we could do it all ourselves."

Laura smiled, glad Mia was powering ahead with ambitious plans. The process of putting the film together had been grueling, not helped by Joe's decision to quit the team. Mia had handled further shooting herself, as well as editing and general admin. It had left Laura's boss exhausted and, at times, discouraged. But now that they were on the home straight, both women felt sure they had a hit on their hands.

"Hey," Laura said. "Let's check out the website. We need an ego boost after slogging through all this stuff. And we could float the new, restrained title, see what the fans think."

Mia agreed, and they were soon scrolling through comments from fans of the series. The news coverage of Rookwood had created huge interest in earlier episodes of Great British Hauntings. Of course, there was the usual percentage of brickbats, and Laura skimmed by them, sighing at the semi-literate abuse.

"Hey, hold on," said Mia. "We shouldn't ignore our critics."

Laura sighed again, louder this time. Another characteristic of Mia was she was obsessed with feedback, in all its forms. Dutifully she scrolled back up, through the latest cluster of craziness. For some reason, one adverse or just plain bonkers comment always seemed to attract more of the same.

"Like flies on a dung heap," she murmured.

Mia said nothing, but rolled her chair forward a little, peered at the screen.

"Not just our regular haters and nutcases," she said. "I thought there was something else. See? It's changing. Tone and content."

Laura had only glanced at the comments before scrolling past them, looking for something positive. She had seen a few keywords— evil, deranged, sick—and naturally assumed they were hostile. But in fact, as she read more carefully, things were not so clear cut. Some people were full of praise and enthusiasm. But not necessarily for Great British Hauntings.

Palmer—sick! What a brilliant guy.

'Deranged'? Yeah, like Einstein was deranged. Man was a genius. Respect!

What people seem to forget is that Palmer was clearly part of a great tradition of true visionaries, dating back at least as far as the Order of the Golden Dawn, who sought to marry scientific methods to the so-called occult.

These were all, Laura decided, par for the course. People online had a tendency to miss the moral in any story, even the most straightforward.

"If Hitler was on Twitter, he'd get thousands of Likes," she pointed out. "It makes me despair for our species, just a little."

"Yeah," Mia concurred, "but look here. And here."

Laura looked. Some commenters had gone well beyond moral ambiguity or indifference about Palmer's activities. They were downright creepy in their adoration.

The Palmer entity is the god these insane times demand. Frightening? Evil? Perhaps. A vengeful god, a mad god, a god that acquires its own sacrifices. There is a dark poetry in it all.

Doctor Miles Rugeley Palmer, like a true messiah, was martyred by a treacherous disciple, but rose from the dead to take his followers forward. The difference is this messiah is alive now, in a real place. Don't accept that bullshit about him being destroyed for a second.

These are the first days of the New Church, the New Faith. Palmerism, we could call it. I would happily be absorbed into his essence. Shit, what is there to live for in this lousy world?

As for his supposed evil, give me a break! Our corrupt governments and multinational corporations kill more people every day than he 'murdered' over decades.

Maybe in Palmer, we've finally found a Power that could bring down this Brutal New World Order...

There were dozens of similar comments, ranging from the obvious tongue-in-cheek trolling to apparently sincere claims of devotion. Palmer had worshippers—smart ones, it seemed. Otherwise normal people who had become fascinated by the story, but not in the way Mia had expected. Laura hoped they were just a few, fairly typical internet crazies, and said so.

"Well," Mia said, in a slightly subdued tone, "you know how keen the public is on death, cruelty, the darker side of our natures. This is really not much different from those people who want to marry serial killers. Notoriety is fame, and we live in a fame-obsessed culture."

"We're making Palmer a global celebrity," Laura said flatly. "A mad doctor with a god complex. Is that a good thing?"

"Pshaw," Mia said, standing up and stretching. "We can't stop now we're nearly ready to go. And like you always say, the nutters are outweighed by the nice, sane people. Most of the time. Now, let's grab some lunch before my brain implodes. After all, it's not like the old bastard is around anymore. Nothing's happened at Rookwood since the big bang."

***

When classes at Tynecastle resumed, Paul met Mike for lunch. Today, they had both grabbed a sandwich and gone for a stroll in the small park near the college.

"Indian summer," Mike said, with a very British desire to discuss the weather. "You see, that's an American term. We used to call this kind of autumn heatwave 'St Martin's summer'. It's a classic example of cultural colonization. Old Percy used to get quite upset about that kind of thing. Ironic, given our own history."

They fell silent for a few moments, then Mike asked Paul how his search for work was going.

"I still get questions about, quote, 'demonic possession,'" Paul replied. "But I'm hoping it will blow over. People get bored so quickly, nowadays. There's always some new distraction."

"No more ghosts among the bright young things?" asked Mike, nodding at groups of students strolling, lunching, playing frisbee.

Paul shook his head.

"Unwanted gift has been returned, so that's a small mercy."

"No more bad dreams? Full disclosure," Mike went on, "I haven't heard any screaming at night, so I'm guessing not."

Paul had to laugh at that.

"Nothing I can remember," he said. "Some dreams about my mom, which are not fun, but I've always had those."

They came to a seat that had just been vacated and quickly claimed it. City pigeons began to bob their way toward them as they took out their lunches. The sheer normality of the scene helped Paul quell some doubts. It was hard to believe so many people, such an apparently stable world, could be threatened by something so bizarre as the long-dead Palmer, whatever form he took.

A pink frisbee skimmed low and ricocheted off Paul's thigh. Mike stooped, scooped up the plastic disc, and flung it with energy but little skill back at a couple of laughing girls.

"That's a failing grade, Sara," he shouted.

"Sod off, Mike," came the cheerful reply.

"I see they still respect you as much as ever," Paul remarked.

"It's wonderful to be worshipped," Mike said, then looked serious. "Do you really think Palmer merged with—whatever that forest god was called when people knew its name? Because we've not seen anything that suggests the entity is still around, not since Percy's death."

"I think Palmer tried, and maybe he partially succeeded, but whatever new gestalt entity he botched together came apart after a while," said Paul. "And then his last hurrah, as you put it, was killing a poor old man who had helped us defeat him. Cruel and ultimately futile, but that's in character."

They ate in silence for a while, then discussed everyday matters. After they finished, they got up to amble back to the college. Along the way, they passed a war memorial to a local regiment that had gone to fight in 1914. Paul had often wondered about the poetry engraved on the bronze plaque and mentioned it to Mike.

"'How sleep the brave who sink to rest, by all their country's wishes blest...'" the Englishman quoted. "Nothing to do with the First World War, in fact—it's from an eighteenth-century poem by William Collins about the sinking of a battleship. In peacetime, pure accident. But the words were still apt enough, it seems."

Paul thought about the sleep of the dead, the assumption that those who passed on went to an eternal rest. He knew better. But he hoped Liz, at least, had found peace in some form. If not the conventional heaven, then at least a kind of nirvana, where all suffering was banished.

She might have lied to me, he thought, *but faced with her choices, who would have done differently? And as for Palmer, well, who cares where he's gone.*

Epilogue

The screams woke Neve from a deep, dreamless sleep. At first, she thought there was a drunken fracas in the street, or an elderly, insomniac neighbor had their TV turned up too loud. But these thoughts flashed by in the fraction of a second it took her to recognize her daughter's voice. She almost collided with Ella, and scooped her up, amazed at her own strength. She brought the child into her bed, not asking any questions, merely holding the girl and waiting for the crying to stop.

It was four in the morning before she had teased out a description of the nightmare. During the long process, Neve had prayed it would be about anything other than Liz. When the truth finally emerged, she was startled, then slightly embittered. She felt, not for the first time, that God was not playing fair with them.

"It was about Annie," Ella explained. "It was about a really bad thing Annie did."

It took her a few seconds to remember who Annie was. Annie Elizabeth Semple, the teenager sent to Rookwood. Palmer's most gifted victim, the girl with amazing telekinetic powers. The patient who had finally killed the doctor and caused the first fire in the East Wing.

"I don't understand, honey," she said. "Didn't Liz stop being Annie after—well, after she died? She became a new person, a stronger one. Right?"

"Yes," conceded Ella, with a sniffle. "But there was a time when she was still Annie, doing all sorts of bad things. Because she hated people for sending her to that place, giving her to that man. He played with her like she was his pet, but not in the nice way you're supposed to treat pets."

Neve tried not to shudder at the thought, tried to find a way to take her daughter's mind off the dream. She told herself it was a kind of confabulation, not the product of genuine contact with Liz, Annie, whatever she was called. She put this idea into the plainest words she could find and tried to get Ella to accept it.

"No," said the girl stubbornly. "I know what bad dreams are like. This was something else."

Ella pulled back and looked up at her mother. The bedside light was on, banishing the darkness, but now it let Neve see how tormented Ella's eyes were. She felt ashamed at having tried to dismiss the terrible vision imposed on her sleeping child. Whatever it had been, it was as real as anything else linked to Rookwood.

"She's still trapped there," Ella said. "She thought she would be free. She was going to move on once the link to that place was gone, that's why she told him to destroy it. But when the link was cut, she was carried on by—something like the ocean. It was cold and mean, and it was like she was drowning, forever. And then she was in Hell, and Hell is a lot like Rookwood, the bad old Rookwood, where they put her when she was alive. She wants us to pray for her, mummy, because she thinks that might help. And to tell Paul."

Neve froze. Her recent religious doubts had extended to Heaven, and to God's mercy. But Hell, she had always believed in. Hell was real. She'd seen it in the eyes of at least one man.

"But why?" she asked, whispering urgently, as if someone might overhear. "You said yourself, honey, she was the victim."

"When she was still Annie, she hurt some boys. It was a bad thing, and she realized then that she was crazy and had to stop lashing out. And then she became Liz, and she pretended Annie hadn't done really bad things."

"She killed children?"

Neve knew her own eyes must be as wide as Ella's now, filled with horror. They were no longer mother and daughter, but two motionless girls in a pool of light in the vastness of night.

In the world's shadow.

Ella recited some names, three old-fashioned names that might well have been given to boys in or around World War Two. Neve lay hugging her child until the night was banished, and then did her best to get her ready for school, relieved to see Ella's limbs bore no marks. Whatever else had happened, Liz had not managed to take possession of the girl, or at least not for long enough to matter.

After she had taken Ella to school Neve came home and decided to lose herself in her work. But every time she tried to get started, the names came back to her. Eventually, she gave up and did a quick internet search. Online archives of local newspapers provided confirmation.

BOYS FOUND DEAD IN GROUNDS OF ABANDONED ASYLUM

"So she's in Hell, because she's a murderer."

Neve sat back in her chair, wondering if Palmer, too, had been sent for similar punishment. It would be just. But then she thought of Palmer's victims, absorbed into the entity he had become. Could they all be considered culpable for wrongs done at his volition?

"Above my pay grade," she muttered, getting back to her work. "Just so long as the bastard's gone for good."

***

"Three thousand pound a metric ton," said Baz. "Stripped the insulation from the bright metal, dead easy with these new machines, so it's money for old rope."

Carl suppressed the impulse to ask how copper wires could also be old rope.

"Yeah, right," he said. "But what's that got to do with me?"

Baz, moving quickly for an old guy, clipped Carl around the left ear.

It was a mild blow, but it reminded Carl his uncle had a reputation in Tynecastle's criminal underworld. The scrap dealer was well known to the police, in fact, he was on first name terms with quite a few of them. Carl had not wanted to work for Baz, but his mother had insisted he 'get out of the bloody house and earn some money'.

"What it's got to do with you, you daft article," Baz said in his special low-and-menacing voice, "is that some local toe rags tried to nick this stuff from Rookwood before that Yank blew the place up. They ended up killing each other instead of doing the job—nobody knows why. But it makes me a bit nervous."

Carl looked at the heaps of gleaming wire piled up in the corner of the shed. It seemed innocent enough, but the mention of Rookwood made him nervous. Everybody said the place was haunted, and that the police were lying about what had happened there. Two lads he had known from school had died there.

"You think it might be possessed or something?" he asked innocently. "I totally get that."

This time the blow to the side of his head set his ears ringing.

"Possessed? Don't be bloody stupid! I'm talking about some other little twerps, not unlike yourself, breaking in to nick the wire. Steal my profits. I paid a nice little bribe to a certain sub-contractor to get that wire. And now I need you to sit here, like the dimwitted pudding you are, and guard it overnight."

No way, thought Carl. *You can shove your job where the sun don't shine, I don't care what Mum says, I'm not stopping here after dark.*

But somehow the words did not come out, and half an hour later he was sitting in the shed with a torch and a packet of sandwiches as night came down in the heart of the city. He played on his phone for a while, complained about his treatment via social media, got mocked by his friends, then found his battery was down to three percent. And he had no charger. Cursing, he tried playing with the torch instead, making rabbit ears, then tried to create his own silhouette porno on the wall of the shed. He soon discovered his creative powers were much more limited than his imagination, and simply sat, drifting in and out of sleep as the chill of night closed in.

"Hey, Carl."

He nearly fell out of the rickety folding chair, jumped up, and shone the torch wildly around the shed. The beam glanced off copper coils, settled on a hideously distorted face that seemed to be growing out of the cracked concrete of the shed's floor. It took him a second to realize it was just a crumpled old sack.

"Carl, over here."

He spun around and froze as the flashlight illuminated a skinny, short figure in the opposite corner. The hood was pulled up, the head bowed so no face was visible. But there was something familiar about the stranger.

"Warren?" he said tentatively.

It took him another moment to remember Warren was one of the two guys who had died at Rookwood. Died violently. Then he was stumbling backward, clawing at the door handle. The door opened as soon as he put weight onto it, and he fell to the ground. The torch flew from his fingers and rolled, splashing light uselessly onto the locked gates of the scrapyard.

"Carl, no need to run. Plenty of time. No hurry."

He looked up, saw another large shape looming over him. Again, the voice rang a bell.

"Dwayne? Dwayne, mate, let me go, I promise I won't tell—I won't do anything."

Warren, just visible in the gloom, emerged from the shed, squatted by Carl. Dwayne hunkered down on his other side. He could just make out their pale, oval faces in the diffuse light from the streetlamps. He was glad he could not see them more clearly.

"Let you go?"

Warren reached out a hand that was almost complete, patted Carl on the cheek. His fingers were bony and ice-cold.

"Let you go to do what? To go on being bossed around by that

156

arsehole Baz? To do what mummy tells you? To be laughed at by girls, sneered at by your so-called friends? Face it, Carl—you'll be better off with us."

All Carl's misery seemed to well up inside him, every atom of self-doubt, shame, and cowardice swamping his instinct for self-preservation. Warren was right. Warren had always been clever. Warren and Dwayne were dead, and they were doing all right, that seemed clear enough.

He stood up, the growing chill wrapping around him like a garment. All the while Warren continued to murmur into his ear, with Dwayne making occasional affirmative noises.

"That's right, pal. You're getting in on the ground floor of this one, and it's a big friggin' deal. You're special—he's really choosey about who he takes. For now, anyway."

Carl felt special, suddenly sure that life—life as he knew it, anyway—was not for him. Dwayne took him by one arm, Warren by the other, and they led him into the shed. Through the dirty window, he saw the copper wire had partially untangled itself, and was already snaking over a roof beam, displacing cobwebs, sending down a little shower of dust. A noose was forming, shining in the darkness. The folding chair righted itself, slid across the floor, and stopped under the loop of bright metal.

"Let us help you up, mate."

* * *

If you enjoyed the book, please leave a review. Your reviews inspire us to continue writing about the world of spooky and untold horrors!

Check out these best-selling books from our talented authors

Ron Ripley (Ghost Stories)
- Berkley Street Series Books 1 – 9
  www.scarestreet.com/berkleyfullseries
- Moving in Series Box Set Books 1 – 6
  www.scarestreet.com/movinginboxfull

A. I. Nasser (Supernatural Suspense)
- Slaughter Series Books 1 – 3 Bonus Edition
  www.scarestreet.com/slaughterseries

David Longhorn (Sci-Fi Horror)
- Nightmare Series: Books 1 – 3
  www.scarestreet.com/nightmarebox
- Nightmare Series: Books 4 – 6
  www.scarestreet.com/nightmare4-6

Sara Clancy (Supernatural Suspense)
- Banshee Series Books 1 – 6
  www.scarestreet.com/banshee1-6

For a complete list of our new releases and best-selling horror books, visit www.scarestreet.com/books

See you in the shadows,
Team Scare Street

Made in the USA
Middletown, DE
03 August 2023

36018860R00091